BOSS'S BABY SURPRISE

AVA GRAY

Copyright © 2024 by Ava Gray

All rights reserved.

No part of this book may be reproduced in any form or by any electronic or mechanical means, including information storage and retrieval systems, without written permission from the author, except for the use of brief quotations in a book review.

❦ Created with Vellum

ALSO BY AVA GRAY

CONTEMPORARY ROMANCE

Mafia Kingpins Series

His to Own

His to Protect

His to Win

The Valkov Bratva Series

Stolen by the Bratva

Harem Hearts Series

3 SEAL Daddies for Christmas

Small Town Sparks

Her Protector Daddies

AVA GRAY

Her Alpha Bosses

The Mafia's Surprise Gift

The Billionaire Mafia Series

Knocked Up by the Mafia

Stolen by the Mafia

Claimed by the Mafia

Arranged by the Mafia

Charmed by the Mafia

Alpha Billionaire Series

Secret Baby with Brother's Best Friend

Just Pretending

Loving The One I Should Hate

Billionaire and the Barista

Coming Home

Doctor Daddy

Baby Surprise

A Fake Fiancée for Christmas

Hot Mess

Love to Hate You - The Beckett Billionaires

Just Another Chance - The Beckett Billionaires

Valentine's Day Proposal

The Wrong Choice - Difficult Choices

The Right Choice - Difficult Choices

SEALed by a Kiss

The Boss's Unexpected Surprise

Twins for the Playboy

When We Meet Again

The Rules We Break

Secret Baby with my Boss's Brother

Frosty Beginnings

Silver Fox Billionaire

Taken by the Major

Daddy's Unexpected Gift

Off Limits

Playing with Trouble Series:

Chasing What's Mine

Claiming What's Mine

Protecting What's Mine

Saving What's Mine

The Beckett Billionaires Series:

Love to Hate You

Just Another Chance

. . .

Standalone's:

Ruthless Love

The Best Friend Affair

PARANORMAL ROMANCE

Maple Lake Shifters Series:

Omega Vanished

Omega Exiled

Omega Coveted

Omega Bonded

Everton Falls Mated Love Series:

The Alpha's Mate

The Wolf's Wild Mate

Saving His Mate

Fighting For His Mate

Dragons of Las Vegas Series:

Thin Ice

Silver Lining

A Spark in the Dark

Fire & Ice

Dragons of Las Vegas Boxed Set (The Complete Series)

Standalone's:

Fiery Kiss

Wild Fate

BLURB

He was my boss, my first love, and my baby's father.

Six years later, he's back—and doesn't even remember me.

Landed dream internship with billionaire architect? Absolutely.

Swept away by a dangerous silver fox? You know it.

Secret pregnancy and shattered dreams? That's my life.

I thought I was building my future. Instead, I became a single mom with my career on hold.

Now Kyle Love is back—arrogant genius, walking red flag, and clueless father of my child.

He's ready to buy my firm and rekindle our spark. But when the truth comes out, all hell breaks loose.

Can we rebuild our shattered past, or will his ego and my secrets tear us apart?

One thing's certain—juggling motherhood, office politics, and a silver fox more tempting than the corner office won't be easy.

Boss's Baby Surprise is a steamy contemporary romance with a guaranteed HEA! Packed with your favorite tropes: billionaire, secret baby, second chance, office romance, and age gap. This sizzling story features a curvy heroine and a silver fox hero who will keep you turning pages late into the night.

1

CLARISSA

"You aren't wearing that, are you?" my roommate asked.

I looked down at my outfit. I thought I looked good. Presentable, as my mother would say.

"What's wrong with what I'm wearing?" I fingered the side of my skirt. It was vintage, A-line, light purple, mini-wale corduroy, very office friendly, or at least I thought it was.

"Nothing if you're a fifty-year-old librarian. I thought you said you got an internship at an architectural firm," Marci continued.

"I did." I pressed my hands down the front of the vest I wore. It was also vintage, really old, from some big guy's tux. It fit really well over my chest, but even I had to take a few stitches to nip in the sides. I was curvy, but not as curvy as whoever this had been made for.

"So why are you dressed like your mother? More realistically, like how your mother probably dressed for her first job in the last century!"

I let out a heavy sigh. Marci was so dramatic. The last century wasn't all that long ago. So what if I had never lived in it? I was wearing vintage, so thirty-plus years was to be expected.

"You were in the same seminar as I was," I started.

"The one where they told us how to dress for work? Yeah, but she didn't say you had to dress hyper-conservative, just not to wear your slutty clubbing clothes. You look…" Marci shook her head as she pushed off the junky couch we had rescued off the side of the road and walked around me, plucking at my clothes.

"Sweater *or* vest, not both. The skirt could be cute, but it really doesn't do much for your figure."

"It covers my hips."

"Yeah, like a tarp. It's just there. If it says anything, it's saying, 'look, big hips here.'"

"It's not meant to be a statement piece. That's the vest," I pointed out.

"Then let the vest be a statement piece and don't hide it under the sweater."

She reached up and pulled my sweater off. "Really, Clarissa? That shirt?"

With a grunt of exasperation, Marci stomped off to the bedroom we shared. It was a small room with our perspective beds lining opposite walls and a single closet we had crammed with all of our clothes. But we had an off-campus apartment. I know I thought we had achieved optimal city living.

Marci was already pulling a few items out of the closet by the time I dragged myself in behind her.

"Tell me everything you know about this architecture firm," she said as she dumped clothing on my bed, and then, with her hands on her hips, she looked back at me.

"It's the Love Agency," I said. I emphasized the name. Kyle Love was a big deal. And the fact that I had been selected as one of the summer interns was going to set me up for a great job after I graduated.

"Okay, so what's love architecture? Is that a style, or something dirty?"

"Kyle Love," I said.

"That means nothing to me. I don't take architecture classes."

"Kyle Love is one of the hottest architects in the world. He has buildings all over the place—Dubai, Hong Kong, London."

Marci nodded. "Okay, how old is he?"

I shrugged. "I don't know. I don't think he's what I would call old-old."

Marci rolled her eyes. "Forty and over, or under forty?"

"Probably under. Why?"

Marci shook her hands at me. "Why? Because you are wearing old people's clothes, Clarissa."

"Vintage," I corrected.

"Vintage doesn't automatically make it cool. You look like you expect to go to work for a bunch of old grandpas. If this Kyle Love guy is a big deal, he's not going to trust some middle-aged librarian looking chick to be able to design anything other than kitchen cabinets."

I bit my top lip. Marci knew my reluctance to embrace body positivity and show off my figure. Every time I tried, it had a bad habit of smacking me in the face. I knew I tended to hide behind my clothes. "I don't want to have too much attention on my clothes."

"I understand. But you're going into an industry where people will look at you and judge. If you can't put effort into how you look, how can they trust you will put effort into your designs?"

"That's what my portfolio is for," I said.

"Yeah, but they have to get past you to be interested in seeing your portfolio. You don't have to be all 'look at me', but you can't hide behind frumpy old clothes, either." She turned and picked up a plain shirt and held it up in front of me. "Pick one, the skirt or the vest."

This was one battle I wasn't going to win. In the end, I showed up to my first day interning at the Love Agency in the purple skirt and the sweater I'd originally planned on wearing, only this time, it was as my blouse. A wide belt gave me the appearance of having an hourglass shape. Marci insisted I wear my Doc Martin boots, not dress shoes.

I had to admit, after seeing how the rest of my intern cohort showed up on our first day, I was very glad Marci had helped. I wasn't in anything that called attention to my body, and I looked relatively stylish. On a scale of fashion to frumpy, I was closer to the frumpy end. I never was going to be like the two women in the group who were built and dressed like models, but at least I wasn't like the guy who looked like he had slept in his clothes last night.

There were six of us crammed into a conference room with boxes of catered coffee. Steve, the guy who looked like he had rolled out of bed and straight here, sat hunched over a cup of coffee. The models, Bella and Kendall, hovered in a corner with their phones out, talking quietly to each other. Occasionally, they would glance out at the rest of us. The other two guys, Conner and a second guy named Steve, discussed some sporting event that happened over the weekend.

I sat across from the tired looking Steve and examined my cuticles. I didn't want to play with my phone, thinking that might make a bad impression. And I didn't drink coffee. Without anything to do, the wait seemed infinite.

Alayna Hunt, the woman I had interviewed for the internship with, stepped into the office with the most gorgeous man I had ever seen right behind her.

"Good morning, everyone," Alayna announced. "Welcome. We're so glad you're here with us. This is the Love Agency's inaugural year of having a summer internship program. We hope this experience proves to be as valuable to your future as we believe your fresh perspectives will bring to us."

Steve made a half-awake noise. I glanced over at him and saw him blink and try to focus. He lurched, and I was afraid he was going to be sick.

"Are you okay?" I whispered, but I don't think Steve noticed.

The handsome man with Alayna crossed the conference room and stood behind Steve, clasping his hands onto Steve's shoulders. "Time to wake up and join us here, okay, bud?" The man put the back of his hand against Steve's neck. "Dude, you are burning up. You should have called in sick. Alayna, take this guy to see if you can get him someplace to rest, or see if he needs to go to a doctor."

He hooked his arm under Steve's armpit and hauled him to his feet. "Alayna is going to get you taken care of."

"Of course." Alayna took Steve, and they left.

The models in the corner twittered, and Conner and the other Steve made some cough-insult about blowing his chance on the first day.

The handsome man turned to me and asked, "Do you happen to have any hand sanitizer?"

I nodded, my tongue unable to work in this man's presence, and grabbed my purse. I squirted hand sanitizer into his waiting palm.

"Thank you." He turned to everyone else. "I had a whole speech prepared for you this morning, but I guess that got usurped. Hi, welcome. I'm Kyle Love. I guess this brings up some expectations the agency is going to have of you. You can't do good work if you are not healthy. Someone, probably the internship coordinator at that young man's school, convinced him to show up no matter what. If you're sick, please call in. If you do not have Alayna's number in your phone by now, make sure you do before the end of the day."

He kept rubbing his hands together. "I touched him. I'll be right back, I've got to wash my hands."

Kyle Love strode from the conference room.

Suddenly, the conversations in the room grew in volume. The models—I really was going to have to think of them by their names—exclaimed at how attractive Kyle was while the guys joked about poor Steve blowing his chance here.

I sat there and kept reliving the moment Kyle looked into my eyes and asked for hand sanitizer. His eyes were the most amazing pool blue. I could have drowned in them. I could have stared into his face for hours and not gotten bored or distracted.

He had the kind of cheek bones that sculptors graced their depictions of the gods with to convey their higher earthly origins and ethereal beauty. He had a jawline that wouldn't stop. And he had asked me for hand sanitizer.

I bit my upper lip and closed my eyes. I really hoped I hadn't done anything so embarrassing as blushing. I let out a long breath and hoped that I wouldn't flare up in a blush when and if Kyle Love returned.

2

KYLE

layna leaned on my desk. Her hip had her almost sitting. She watched over the tablet as I scrolled through the digital sketches from the interns.

"I like this one," she said as I swiped, and a new design displayed.

For a sketch, the lines were clean and precise. The idea was clear and creative. "It's good. Who did it?"

I lifted my eyes to her. She oversaw the interns and their projects. I was in and out of the office too much to know too much more than the personalities I had mentally assigned them—the Frat Boys, the Party Girls, Sick Steve, and Clarissa.

"That's Clarissa's," Alayna said.

"Clarissa? She's the... quiet one?" I had to stop myself from saying something else, like the curvy one. Clarissa was quiet, but she was also perfectly lovely. She had beautiful curves and lips that inspired dirty thoughts. And I didn't think she even realized it.

I took a deep breath and girded my unintentional thoughts. My first thoughts regarding Clarissa had no place in an office setting. A bedroom? Yes, but not here. Not here.

"Are all her sketches like this?"

"Yeah, she's got raw talent. Keep going. Check out the next one."

Another well thought out and executed sketch appeared.

"Clarissa again?" I asked.

Alayna shook her head. "Steve did this one."

"Steve? Which one?"

"Steve from University of Illinois, Chicago," she answered.

"Sick Steve?" I asked.

"You did not just call him that." Alayna laughed.

I shook my head, suppressing a chuckle. "You don't want to know what I call the other Steve in my head."

"You're right, I don't. And for the record, I don't want to know your internal monologue about me."

"I don't have an internal monologue about you. I know your name. The nicknames are so I remember," I said.

"Do I even want to know how you remember our clients?" she teased.

"Clients are easy. Their names are on the checks." I returned my attention to the drawings. "Okay, I know who I want. The Party Kids can be in one team, and I want Clarissa and Sick Steve working together with me."

Alayna picked up the tablet and stood. "Got it. 'The Party Kids' is an accurate description, but you're going to have to stop calling him 'Sick Steve'. Who do you want to meet with first?"

"Set up a lunch with the kids, and then I want lunch and a full afternoon blocked off for Clarissa and Steve."

"Lunch with kids before you leave so I can get them assigned, and an afternoon with the other interns when you get back?"

"Sounds good."

Within a few minutes, I had a calendar confirmation for the first lunch on Thursday. I didn't put any more thought into the interns for the rest of the day, and halfway through the next day, until I overheard a conversation I shouldn't have.

"Did you notice Kyle didn't invite Clarissa or Steve?" It was one of the party girls.

"I feel so bad for them. They are trying so hard. It's clear they just aren't cut out for this. Do you see how she dresses? She needs to do something about her weight if she wants to be taken seriously."

"This is gonna be lit. Steve and Conner are so cute, and we're going to be working in a special group with them," the other one said. I think it was Kendall.

"Shut up, here comes Clarissa."

They were quiet for a moment and then they were talking again.

"Hi, Clarissa, have you heard anything else from Alayna about these projects?" Kendall said with a certain sneer in her voice.

"No, not yet. But she had mentioned we would be divided into groups. I'm sure that's all it is," Clarissa said. She was quieter than usual and sounded sad.

My gut bunched. I did not want Clarissa to be sad, and I very much did not want her to think I wasn't impressed with her work. Eavesdropping was middle school behavior, but there I was like some kid, sneaking around my own firm.

"Ladies, how is everyone this morning?" I greeted them loudly and with a hint of too much enthusiasm. The party girls twittered with giggles. "Kendall, Bella, I look forward to our lunch tomorrow.

Clarissa"— her eyes were cast down, and when she looked up at me through her lashes, I had visions of her looking up at me for very different reasons— "come with me. We should chat about your sketches."

I kept walking, and Clarissa took several rapid steps to catch up.

"What? Of course, yes. I'm sorry if they—"

"Never apologize for your sketches. More people need to be able to draw as cleanly as you do."

Behind us, the party girls were continuing to giggle and gossip in the hall.

"I wanted to make sure that you and Steve knew what was going on," I continued.

"Well, I figured Alayna divided us into groups based on something," Clarissa said. "But she didn't say anything to me, so I don't know."

I stepped into an empty conference room and held the door open so she could step in. I closed the door and indicated that she should have a seat.

"Am I being fired from the program?" she asked before I took a seat.

"What? No. Why do you think that?"

She wouldn't look at me, and she kept sucking her upper lip behind her lower one. I saw the white tips of her teeth as she bit herself. She shrugged and shook her head. She looked up, but her gaze landed somewhere over my shoulder. "The lunch on Thursday thing. And I think Bella and Kendall might know something they aren't telling me."

Clarissa let out a dejected sigh.

I grabbed the arms of her chair and pulled it so that she had to look at me. "That's not what's happening. The interns have been divided into two groups. I'm having lunch with the group on Thursday before they are assigned to shadow different aspects of the firm. I have a meeting

BOSS'S BABY SURPRISE

out of the country, and I leave on Friday. We wanted to get that group situated right away. I'm surprised Alayna hasn't already scheduled us for when I get back. You and Steve will be working with me when I get back."

She blinked a few times, and her large eyes seemed to get even bigger. "Wha… what? Are you serious?"

I sat back and nodded. Seeing her happy brought a smile to my face. "You are definitely not getting fired. You have real talent. I mean, the entire intern cohort does, but your drawing skills at the sketch level are exceptional. I can see what you are thinking. I don't need you to explain what I'm looking at or to redraw it to clarify a concept. Alayna may not have said anything yet to spare the egos of the rest of the group."

"Are you serious?" She practically vibrated in her seat.

And then, rather unexpectedly, she launched herself at me. Her arms swung up and around my neck, and she pressed her soft breasts against my chest.

She let go and jumped away just as quickly. "I shouldn't have done that. Sorry, sorry. I really thought I was being fired from the program. Oh, God, you're not going to fire me now because I hugged you?"

I still felt the hot press of her body against mine. I don't think she realized she had grabbed onto my hand and kept shaking it with excitement.

"I won't say a thing. Your enthusiasm is refreshing. You might want to curb that when it comes to working with others in the firm."

She twisted around nervously. "I know better, I really do. No hugging at work. But oh, my God, this is amazing. Can I tell Steve? I'll swear him to secrecy."

She lifted her hands to shake mine in her glee. Her gaze landed on our clasped hands as she noticed my hand in hers. She dropped me like a hot potato. "Sorry, sorry." And then she lit up like a neon sign, blushing.

She clamped her hands over her face. "Don't say anything, you'll just make it worse," she groaned.

I laughed. She was adorable, and I shouldn't have found her enthusiasm quite as attractive as I did. She was my intern. I stuffed down the urge to flirt or comment on how she could touch and hold onto me as much as she wanted.

I cleared my throat. "I won't say anything about that vibrant blush"—even though I wanted to know how far down her pale skin it went—"if you stop apologizing for everything."

She lowered her hands and blinked at me. Her cheeks were still flushed. "Sorry." The blush returned with a burst like a solar flare, and she was back behind her hands.

I couldn't help but sit and laugh, not at her, but at the situation. I hadn't worked with anyone so excited in a long time. It was refreshing. I had forgotten how to have that kind of enthusiasm over work.

I looked up when Alayna knocked and walked into the conference room. "I take it you told her? Congratulations, Clarissa."

Clarissa lowered her hands and looked at Alayna with wide eyes.

"I overheard some comments from the other interns and came to make sure you knew what was really going on," Alayna said.

"Does Steve know?" Clarissa asked.

Alayna shook her head.

"I'm going to go tell him. I won't say anything to anyone else. I'll pretend to be sad," Clarissa said as she darted out of the conference room.

"I doubt that girl can pretend to be sad. She's happy with her entire body." Alayna chuckled as she watched Clarissa scurry away.

"Uh-huh," I said as I stared after Clarissa, admiring the way her backside moved.

"You like her, don't you?"

"Of course, I like her. She is wholeheartedly enthusiastic. We need more of that around here."

3

CLARISSA

"Marci!" I wailed as I returned home after work on Friday.

"I'm right here. What's the matter? Were the mean girls mean again?" She stood in the small kitchen area pouring a pop over some ice.

I had told her about the models and the frat boys and how they weren't exactly the nicest to me. I hadn't told her how Steve and I were going to be shadowing Kyle because I really had a hard time believing it myself.

"The mean girls are so fucking full of themselves. They had lunch with Kyle Love yesterday, and today they spent the first half of the day being condescending twats."

"Clarissa!" Marci exclaimed. "You've been watching too much British TV. You're picking up the bad words."

I flopped onto the couch, my arms and legs spread out like a starfish that gave up all hope. "The bad words are the fun ones." I started spewing all the British slang profanity I could think of. "Bloody, bollox, twat, wanker."

She came and sat next to my sprawled form. "That's it? You came in here whining so you could cuss at me?"

I sat quickly and stared at her like a mad man. "I need an entire new wardrobe, and I have exactly thirty-two dollars in my bank account."

Marci waved her hands around. "Back up there, sunshine. What do the mean girls have to do with your needing new clothes? Do I have to go beat someone up for you?"

I collapsed back with a laugh. "No, but that could be interesting. Bella and Kendall are nothing more than jerks. And they are officially out of my hair. They got their assignments today for the rest of the internship. They're shadowing some drafts-people. They think they're hot shit because they had lunch with Kyle and now have their assignments. And because I wasn't invited to the lunch."

Marci shifted on the couch. "Why not?"

I did a little kick and squirmy dance. "That's the best part," I squealed. "I wasn't invited to one last lunch with the head of the firm because I'm going to be shadowing him."

Marci jumped and was on her knees. "What? No way! This is awesome."

"Right? I know. Steve Kanatas and I were quietly selected so the other interns wouldn't get their panties in a twist, *and* we have a big meeting with Kyle at the end of next week when he gets back from Hong Kong."

"And you want to look cute for Steve?"

"Ew, no. I mean, Steve's not… no. He's cute enough, I guess, but no. I'm going to be working with *Kyle Love*." I emphasized his name. "You know, the freaking head of the whole agency. I cannot accidentally dress like a frumpy librarian around him."

Marci's mouth dropped open into a wide-mouthed smile. "Oh, girl, you have the hots for the boss man."

"Shut up!" I let out a wistful sigh. "Have I mentioned just how incredibly handsome he is?"

"Steve?"

"Kyle!" I went to throw a couch pillow at her but stopped because she had so thoroughly gotten me riled up. I hugged it to my chest and giggled.

"You want to look cute for the boss. How much money did you say you had?"

We spent the weekend going through my closet. With Marci's help, I ended up with twelve outfits I didn't even realize were hiding in the mess of clothes that I already owned. I spent the money I had on buying her dinner as a thank you. It wasn't nearly enough to show my gratitude, but I now had clothes I could wear for the rest of my internship. I didn't need to be super fashionable. I just needed to know that if Kyle looked at me, he wouldn't necessarily think I looked like a potato wearing clothes.

By the time Kyle returned from abroad, my stomach was tied up in knots. I was so nervous. When I walked into the conference room where our meeting was scheduled, I no longer knew if I was anxious because I was going to be one of Kyle Love's interns—an absolute major accomplishment—or because it had been almost a whole week since I had seen him last. Somehow in the past few days, my feelings seemed to have exploded from thinking the boss was hot to having a full-blown crush on the man.

Steve was already sitting staring at the spread of catered sandwiches when I stepped in. Neither Kyle nor Alayna was there yet.

"Are you okay?" Steve asked.

I shook my head with tight movements.

He laughed. "Relax, you'll be fine."

"But we're shadowing Kyle fucking Love," I said. My nerves added a little extra spice to my language. I didn't like cursing at work.

"I practically puked on the guy our first day here, and look at me now. Trust me, Kyle is a good guy."

I slid into a chair. I reached for a napkin and grabbed a bagel. I wasn't hungry, but picking at it gave me something to do. And maybe the bread would soothe my stomach.

"Steve, Clarissa," Kyle exclaimed as he practically burst into the conference room.

I looked for Alayna before letting my gaze land on Kyle. I don't know why I sought out the other woman first as some sort of safe haven for my nerves. She wasn't there, and as soon as my eyes locked with Kyle's, I felt a chill wash over me. A shiver started in my toes and ended at the back of my neck.

He paused before sitting and asked, "Are you all right?"

I nodded frantically. "Excited."

"Excited is good." Kyle turned to Steve. "Are you okay? Not going to be sick?"

Steve laughed. "Not going to be sick. But I'm not nearly as nervous as Clarissa."

Of course he wasn't. He didn't have a crush on the boss like I did.

Kyle eyed the spread of food hungrily and grabbed a plate full of deli sandwich sections and chips. "Well, relax and eat up. I promise there won't be a test at the end of this."

"What are we doing, exactly?" Steve asked.

"Everything." Kyle laughed.

By the end of the hour, we had eaten. Kyle regaled us with tales of architect faux pas, and we ate some more. After a while, we moved the food to a sideboard and Kyle had someone bring in some D-size paper and mechanical pencils.

He rolled the large sheet of paper out on the table and began telling us his ideas. As he spoke, he drew and doodled.

Steve pointed to a part of the drawing. "May I?"

Kyle gave him the go ahead, and Steve began sketching the details as he understood what Kyle was describing.

"That's it! That's exactly why you're here. You took the concept and ran with it," Kyle said, a huge smile on his face.

I got over my nerves once we started drawing. I turned my chair around and kneeled in it so I could reach across the table, having shorter arms than either Kyle or Steve. The building Kyle described developed before our eyes as we communicated through lines and shapes as well as conversation.

The collaborative effort between the three of us was for lack of a better word, fun. I loved being able to talk and joke with people who seemed to really understand how my brain worked. I didn't have to explain simple ideas. I could draw them out, and both of the men knew exactly what I was thinking.

Steve stepped away from the drawing and took a long drink from his cup. All of our drinks were set on the sideboard away from the drawings. He excused himself and stepped out of the room.

With a shrug, Kyle continued to work.

I watched as he seemed to doodle in strenuous details on a patio.

"If you're going to do that, you might as well put in fairy lights," I said as I began to draw in swags of string lights.

Our hands were in close proximity, and our pencils seemed to dance around each other. Kyle bumped my hand, causing me to make a squiggle across the drawing. I glanced up, and he was smirking, so I bumped his hand back. Kyle immediately shifted the paper and created a grid of dots.

I knew this game. It was a race to see who could box off the other person's lines. The next thing I knew, I was giggling, he was laughing, and we were having sloppy scribbling pencil wars.

The next time I looked up at him, it felt like all the air had been sucked out of the room. His smile melted and I stopped giggling. The laughter was replaced with something much more dramatic and charged. I swear I could feel lightning crackle through the room between us.

"Don't move," Kyle demanded.

I didn't think I could have, even if I wanted to.

He sat down but kept his eyes on me.

I glanced down. His pencil moved with tight, rapid motions.

"No, don't look. Not yet," he said.

"Sorry about that," Steve said as he stepped back into the conference room.

Kyle cleared his throat and tore a corner from the sheet of paper we had been drawing on. He folded the section and tucked it into his pocket.

I eased back off the table. My knees were still on my chair, but I was practically lying across the conference table to be closer to Kyle while we were being silly.

"Anything good develop while I was indisposed?" Steve asked.

I tried not to blush.

"I beat Clarissa at snakes," Kyle announced.

"You did not. I totally boxed you in," I declared.

Kyle leveled a calm, even look at me. There was no hint of that charged moment between us in his eyes, but I swear I felt something in his words. "I challenge you to a rematch."

4

KYLE

I watched Alayna leave my office, her arms full of rolled up architectural plans. Steve followed behind her like a well-trained puppy, laden down with even more rolled up drawings. We had a client who unfortunately didn't seem to understand my scope of responsibility, and they told their structural engineer to follow up with me regarding aspects of their new building that I had nothing to do with. In typical Alayna fashion, when she brought the problem to me, she already had a solution. She just needed my go ahead to proceed, which meant that I would have free time to work one-on-one with Clarissa this afternoon.

As they left, Clarissa arrived. There was some shuffling of feet as she danced around trying to get out of their way.

"What's that all about?" Clarissa asked after she stepped into my office.

"Somebody else's problem," I replied.

"Oh, yeah? And what exactly is their problem?" She sat down across from me and opened the little black sketchbook she always had with her.

"Are you taking notes?" I asked.

She was always taking notes. This woman was perceptive and tried not to miss any little detail. She looked up at me with a pencil poised over a blank page. "Of course. Always."

I leaned forward on my desk, resting on my elbows "Then write this down," I started. "Get yourself an Alayna. And when you find yourself one, overpay them because they will be worth every penny."

Clarissa scribbled frantically in her notebook.

"Are you telling me I should try to steal Alayna from you when I have my own firm?" She smirked.

"Not at all. More like telling you if they figure out a way to clone her, you need to make sure you get one."

She laughed. It was a delightful tinkling bell sound that made me think fairy magic had to be real. How else could somebody like Clarissa exist? Her smile brought joy, and her presence made me happy for no reason other than she was near. If it wasn't magic, I didn't know what it was.

I was surprised she didn't have wings. I felt like declaring loudly for all to hear, 'I do believe in fairies. I do. I do.'

"So, what's the plan for the rest of the day?" she asked.

I pointed out the door, gesturing toward Alayna and Steve. "Well, Steve has a project with Alayna for the afternoon. That leaves us on our own."

"That could be dangerous," she teased.

She had no idea how dangerous. Especially if I let down my guard. Thoughts ricocheted through my head of just how dangerous I wanted to be with the woman who sat across from me. Thoughts that had nothing to do with sketches of buildings and aesthetic public spaces.

"You have no idea," I said.

Clarissa glanced down, a tinge of pink blushing her cheeks.

"I think I have an idea of how dangerous you could be." Her eyes met mine for a brief second. She bit her lower lip as her gaze darted away from me again.

I eased back in my chair, lacing my fingers and folding my arms to prop my head against my palms.

"How about this? You tell me when it's getting too dangerous for you."

She put her pencil down and closed the sketchbook over it. "I don't know if I should play this game or not, but I'm feeling pretty daring right now."

"Oh, yeah?" I asked.

She continued to chew on her lower lip. Her cheeks grew brighter as she gave me a little nod.

"Then maybe we should take this game out of the office," I announced.

Her eyes went wide, and she swallowed before she nodded.

"Where do you want to take this?" she asked.

I had a short list of where I wanted to take her. Trial by fire, see if she could keep up. My groin tightened, and I felt the primal urge to growl and haul her out of her chair and throw her plump ass over my shoulder before carrying her out of the office and into a cave to ravish her. I clenched my jaw and willed the caveman inside me to calm the fuck down.

Dinner would be nice. I should start with dinner like a civilized man. Even if she didn't make me feel like one.

"Did you want to go over my sketches?" she asked.

I wanted to go over more than just her sketches. Sketches, we could review in the office.

"I want to have one of those conversations where we don't have to worry about who walks in. I want to find out more about you," I admitted.

"Me? I pretty much already told you everything there is to know about me."

Slowly, I shook my head back and forth. "You've told me about your plans for your career. You've told me about your education thus far. But you haven't told me about you. I don't know why you want to become an architect."

She opened her mouth and shifted to speak. I held up my hand, stopping her before she gave me a generic, well-rehearsed answer.

"I have questions that I shouldn't ask while I sit on this side of my desk and you're sitting on that side of it."

"Questions that you could ask sitting across from me at a dinner table?" she asked. Her blush still colored her cheeks.

"Are you asking me out to dinner? Because if you were, I could ask how far down that blush goes? And that's not something I would dare to ask you while we sit here."

She didn't exactly flinch. Her blush grew stronger, and her eyes grew bigger. I could see her shiver like a cornered rabbit. The thought of making her that nervous, instead of deterring me and making me back off, had me wanting her even more.

She stared at me for a long moment before licking her lips. "Dinner could be dangerous."

I smiled, exposing all of my teeth. Skirting the edge of this flirtation was getting me hard. If I was going to be uncomfortable and inappropriate, I didn't want it to be here.

"It's time to take this conversation elsewhere," I announced as I pushed to my feet and stepped around from behind my desk.

Clarissa got to her feet, and I indicated that she should lead the way out. I paused as we passed Alayna's desk. She and Steve were setting up a system organizing the rolls of drawings.

"Looks like you two will be at this for a while," I said.

Alayna gave me a weary sigh. "Yep."

"Make sure you order dinner in," I said. "Feed Steve and charge it back to the client."

"Where are we going?" Clarissa asked nervously.

"Have you ever taken a walking tour of the architecture in Chicago?"

She laughed. It was a genuine laugh. I didn't hear a hint of a nervous giggle. It was a good sign that she had started to relax.

"Of course I have. I've been on many. You can't study architecture in this city and not. Between class field trips and assignments, I could probably give those tours."

"Good. That's what you're going to do. Take me on a walking tour of your favorite architectural details."

She stopped and stared at me. "Are you serious? Right now?" She glanced down at her feet. I followed her gaze.

She had sturdy boots on. She didn't tend toward spindly high heels in her fashion choices. "You can walk in those boots, right?"

She nodded. "To quote Nancy Sinatra, 'These boots are made for walking.' I just can't think of any places to show you."

I lifted my brows. "I thought you said you could give a tour?"

She resumed walking. "I can, but you said of my favorite places. That's different."

"How? Why?"

"Because I have to weigh and judge and think about why I would consider that detail, or that building, one of my favorites. Also, I'm showing you my favorites. Now I have to second guess what your motivation is. Are you judging me based on my choices? What if you absolutely hate my favorites?"

I put my hand on her shoulder to stop her.

She stopped walking and faced me. My hand slid down her arm and rested just above her elbow.

"You're overthinking this. How about showing me five things you might include on a walking tour if you were organizing one? Don't worry about whether or not it's your favorite or if it has historical significance."

"But…"

"You'll explain why you're showing it to me as you're giving your tour. Is that easier?"

She nodded. "Okay, let me get my stuff."

I followed Clarissa to the conference room that had been set up as office space for the interns. She began putting items into an oversized tote bag, including the sketchbook that she took her notes in and an oversized water bottle.

"Do you bring all of that just for work every day?" I asked.

"Gotta stay hydrated," she said, shaking the water bottle at me.

"You could leave your work stuff here, at work," I pointed out. "It's why we gave you an office of sorts."

She shrugged. "I guess I could." As she stared at her tote bag, she twisted her mouth and then bit her lip in what I was learning was an expression of concentration for her.

"Do you really need the sketch book at home? Or the water bottle? You could leave it here and not have to carry it back and forth. Let me guess, you haul in that thing full of water, plus carry a coffee every morning, right?"

"Hey, have you been spying on me?"

I chuckled. "No, but I see other women commuting in, and they are absolutely laden down with too many drinks. Leave the water bottle or get one that's just for work that you can leave. Put down the sketchbook. What else is in that tote bag?"

She pulled something dark out. "A sweater."

"It's unseasonably warm outside and you're bringing a sweater to work?"

"It can get cold in the building," she said.

"Then leave it here," I directed.

5

CLARISSA

My tote bag was considerably lighter as I slung it over my shoulder. Kyle was right, I could leave half of everything I carried back and forth everyday. The water bottle got heavy, and I didn't even start drinking it until I finished my coffee.

I eyed it thoughtfully. It might have been heavy, but we were about to take a long walk on a hot day. I snagged it.

"I thought I convinced you to leave that here?" Kyle chuckled.

"You had, but we're about to go for a walk. I want my water. You should consider getting some too."

"If I get thirsty, I'll stop and buy something," he said.

Why was it that men never seemed to be prepared and women were always over prepared? I had my bag and water, whereas he was literally walking out of the building as he was, unburdened by any extras. It wasn't fair.

I wasn't a fast walker and felt very self-conscious as Kyle strode next to me.

"Where to first?" he asked.

I knew where I wanted to start, and why. Kyle's offices were located in an old industrial building, converted to office spaces during the previous century. We weren't terribly far from where I wanted to be. But it was going to be a walk. Once outside, I headed east, toward the lake.

"Do you know where you're going?" Kyle asked after a few blocks.

"I do. Aren't you up for a walk? This was your idea."

I couldn't see his eyes behind the reflective aviator sunglasses he slipped on, but I imagined he rolled his eyes at me. There was plenty to see of architectural interest, but nothing that I considered worthy of a tour, at least not yet.

A few blocks, and the nature of the buildings surrounding us changed. Skyscrapers began reaching into the sky like a garden of glass and steel. None were quite as tall as Willis Tower, but that was the beauty of the building.

Kyle flipped his hand and pointed in the direction of the tower. "You aren't going to say anything about Willis?"

I shrugged. "No, should I? It's tall. Come on."

We crossed the river, and I kept walking. I tried to hide the fact that I was struggling, huffing and taking overly deep breaths. I should have called a car or flagged a taxi. But Kyle had said walking tour. I was overthinking everything again.

We reached the first location I wanted to show Kyle. I stopped at the corner of East Wacker and North Wabash. "The Jewelers Building. It has these classic revival temples at the top. Fun fact, the ones on the four corners are to hide water tanks. Chicago is full of these rooftop temples. I simply adore them."

I pointed down the street, where the next building I wanted to show

Kyle was clearly visible. "And there's the Tribune Tower. The top of it looks like a Gothic cathedral complete with flying buttresses."

I continued down Wacker and turned onto the bridge before stopping.

"You wanted to show me the DuSable Bridge?" he asked.

"No, I wanted to show you that." I gestured to the buildings we could see more comfortably from where we stood than if we had stopped by their front doors. We stood about halfway over the river on the bridge. "It's the juxtaposition of classical revival next to something some people consider the very definition of modern architecture."

I gestured with my right hand again. "London House, more specifically, the cupola on the roof. It's one of my favorite little gems hidden in the city."

"Have you ever been up there?"

"I've been to the bar, but the cupola is pretty exclusive and in high demand for things like wedding photos and proposals. Every time I'm there, it's closed for a private event," I said.

"Maybe you should reserve it for yourself?" he suggested.

I looked over at him. His head was tipped back as he looked at the roof line. It was just enough to show off the slope of his neck and the bump of his Adam's apple. Dark beard stubble covered the edges of his sharp jaw and neck. I could have stared at him for hours.

I decided that a tour of my favorite view in Chicago would have required handing him a mirror. It wasn't fair how good-looking he was. It felt almost cruel for him to be so funny, nice, and flirty around me.

It took me a long moment of staring at my own reflection in his sunglasses before I clued in that he was looking at me and no longer glancing up at the building.

I cleared my throat and glanced away. "And of course, One Illinois Center," I said as I gestured at the other building.

"Interesting," Kyle said.

"What?"

"That in the midst of your pointing out your love for the revival temples, you also include this one. Now I'm wondering, what is your aesthetic for these choices?"

I grimaced. "Romance versus expectation?"

He returned his gaze back up to the skyscraper. "Okay. Tell me more about expectations."

I let out a bitter laugh. "I'm an architecture student in Chicago. I'm supposed to be enamored with modernism and 'form follows function.'"

"Bauhaus, good," he muttered and nodded.

"Beauty in simplicity, machinery, speed for speed."

"You might be confusing some Futurist concepts in there, but okay." He kept nodding.

I let out a sigh. "Look, I get it. When this style showed up on the scene, it was hot and new, and if I spent my entire life being inundated with the over-the-top ginger-breading of Victorian architecture, I might get giddy looking at the clean lines and functionality of brutalism. You said earlier not to overthink and to show you what I liked and not worry whether you were going to judge me, right?"

He nodded.

"It's a very unpopular opinion to have, and even more so in this field. I'd be laughed out of some classes for not aspiring to be as lean and clean as Mies van der Rohe. But I've grown up with the cheap knock-offs of modern architecture that have bastardized the concepts from something sleek and sexy in design to boring and uninteresting because why bother having visual interest when it just needs to have a door, some interior space, and a roof? I understand the importance of the design of this building, its designer, and its place in time. I can understand that and still find it to be architecturally uninteresting."

"Even in context?" Kyle asked.

"Which context? Nineteen thirty-eight Germany? This would have been unimaginable. Nineteen sixties Chicago, the latest *newest*, a feat of engineering and design. Here, now? It's a big glass box."

I pointed at the four glass and concrete buildings next to it. "So are those." I pointed back to the cupola on top of London House. "And that building has an ancient temple on top of it."

I watched him as he stared at the buildings for a while longer. I knew he had seen them a million times before. He had to have studied them. Hell, he might even be in the school of thought that form follows function was the basis of his designs. He ran his hand over his jaw.

"And the fifth one?" he asked.

I looked around to reorient myself. Looking up at the tops of the buildings had me twisted around. We headed north on Michigan Avenue and then turned west on Superior. I kept walking for blocks, taking sips of my water as we went. We passed apartment buildings and hotels, and then I stopped in front of a small mustard colored row house wedged between apartment high-rises.

Kyle started laughing.

"What?" I asked.

"I should have figured you would have picked this place."

"Why do you say that?" I put my hands on my hips and glared at him. The house was cute. I would have loved to have seen this street when it was full of the old homes.

Kyle held out his hand. "Let me see your sketches."

"You made me leave my sketchbook back at the office, remember?" I tried to be sassy.

"Yeah, but you have your tablet. And that's where you put the sketches you like."

"How do you know that?" I asked. My words came slowly as I fished the tablet out of my bag. I clicked it on, input my password, and then handed it over to him.

I stood next to him and watched over his arm as he scrolled through the gallery of images. He made humming affirmative noises as he scrolled through my sketches.

"This one," he said, holding up something I had redrawn.

It was a cleaned-up version of something I had based on a drawing Steve had done after getting feedback from Kyle. At the time, I felt that Steve had given it good bones, but it needed a little *oomph*.

"You like little gems. Visual surprises. Like this house. Unless you knew it was here, driving down the street, it would completely catch you off guard. And the temples, they are visual gifts, rewarding you for looking up the length of repetitive building façades."

"Nothing wrong with that. There is no visual payoff on half the buildings out there. They are all knock-offs. Exoskeletons aren't new. Glass towers aren't new. Sometimes, it feels like no one is even trying to make new buildings visually interesting."

I shifted my gaze from the tablet to his face. I didn't realize he was so close. He had been looking at me, and now our eyes locked.

"You make things interesting." His voice was low.

When his gaze shifted to my lips, my body tingled like I had been touched. I closed my eyes. His lips against mine were soft, seeking.

"Dangerous," I said with a sigh when he ended the kiss.

6

KYLE

"I mean the man was designing glass-wrapped structures before the building technology was really available. To say it was more than groundbreaking is an understatement. It's almost like he was sent back in time to make sure we got the glittering cities of the future." Steve continued his presentation.

I sat back and half paid attention as Steve went on and on obsessively about Mies van der Rohe's architectural aesthetic. I couldn't help but think how Clarissa's tastes were exactly the opposite. She even admitted hers was not a popular opinion.

In an attempt at treating my interns with equality, I asked Steve to prepare a presentation as if he were going to give me a walking tour of Chicago. He had to pick five pieces and explain why. Pretty much the same assignment I had given Clarissa, only I had no intention of hiking around the city with him. His choices held no surprises for me.

Motion by my open office door caught my attention. I looked as Clarissa tapped on the door frame. "Am I interrupting?"

I let my smile bypass my lips but reach my eyes. I was like some kind of eager puppy whenever I saw her, only it wasn't my tail that started wagging. I waved her in. "Steve was showing me his choices for a walking tour of Chicago. Only, he needs a car to get from place to place."

"You included the Ben Rose house in Highland Park?" she asked.

"Didn't you?" Steve asked.

Clarissa sat in the empty chair next to Steve. "No. Did you include Oak Park or just the Robie House?"

"Oak Park. There are too many Frank Lloyd Wright houses to choose from, so I lumped them all together," he said. "What did you include?"

Clarissa's eyes went wide, and she gave me a panicked look.

"Clarissa's presentation was different. I'm afraid I didn't give her nearly as much time to pull a presentation together. But it was very informative. Are you ready for your next task? I wanted to share some notes on this project and see how you would respond." I proceeded to discuss the details from a project I completed several years earlier. They were being presented with the exact same parameters I had to work with. I knew how I approached and brought resolution to the situation. I wanted to see what their solutions would look like.

As usual, Clarissa took notes, writing down every word I said, while Steve stared at me intently. When we were done, Steve got quiet and began nodding, a lot. That seemed to be his thinking mode. He left without saying much.

Clarissa bit her upper lip and reviewed her notes before making her move.

I waited for her inevitable questions. "Everything okay? Any questions?"

"Of course I'm going to have questions, but nothing is making itself obvious right now."

Her eyes darted away from mine. Ever since the kiss a few days earlier, she was skittish around me. If other people were around, she was calm, and when we were talking business, she was cool and calm. Now that we were alone, she seemed nervous.

I wanted to ease her fears, whatever they were. "I don't bite, Clarissa."

"How do I know? You are dangerous," she said with a small smile.

This time, I let the smile spread over my lips and show off my teeth. "You were pretty daring there, yourself."

"Maybe I like to live on the edge?"

"Then maybe you'd have dinner with me?"

She glanced nervously over her shoulder. "Officially, or…?"

"Let's call it official business," I said.

"Okay, sure."

"Come by when you're ready to go. We can leave from here. Now, you have an assignment to work on."

She nodded and blushed and practically ran out of my office. There was something very sexy about how cute she was. I made a few phone calls. I had plans for tonight.

"Where are we headed?" Clarissa asked as she followed me from the office and into a cab several hours later.

"You'll figure it out soon enough," I said.

It didn't take long before the cab dropped us off. Clarissa looked up the façade of the building. "London House's rooftop bar!" she exclaimed happily. "I haven't been there in ages."

"I know. I thought you'd get a kick out of going up again."

When the elevator doors slid open, I let the hostess know we had special reservations. We didn't have to wait long until we were escorted through the restaurant. Clarissa's hand tightened on my arm as we approached the cupola.

"You didn't?" she whispered.

"I did. You said you always wanted to see it, but it was always closed for a private event. Well, you now have your very own private viewing."

"I can't believe this. Kyle, you're amazing." She let go of my arm and practically skipped up the steps.

In the center, a small table already set with plates waited for us. Clarissa passed it by to lean over the balustrade and look out at the view of the city. Her smile cut straight to my groin.

"It's amazing. The sky from up here... Oh, wow. It looks like a storm is coming in from over the lake." She stepped away from admiring the view and looked up into the dome, spinning in a slow circle. When she stopped, she stared at the table. "Oh, no. They're setting up for dinner. We should probably go before they get here." She pointed at the set table.

"That's for you, for us," I said.

"What? Kyle!" She launched into my arms and pressed her lips to mine.

I sank into her kiss. My arms pulled her tight, and I slid my lips over hers.

Someone coughed and interrupted us.

"Oh, sorry," Clarissa said. Her cheeks glowed pink in the evening light.

She scooted into one of the chairs and took the menu that was offered. I ordered a bottle of wine as I took my menu.

"How did you manage to get a dinner reservation?" Clarissa asked.

"I made a few calls, pulled a few strings." I had gotten lucky. I had intended to see if I could get her a few minutes up here on her own while we ate at the rooftop restaurant. When the concierge I was speaking with about reserving time mentioned they had a dinner cancellation, I took it. Seeing how happy Clarissa was made the effort worthwhile.

Her eyes kept darting around us. Her eyes sparkled with joy. "This is so amazing. But I thought you said dinner would be official. The last thing I want to do right now is talk about building sketches and calculating external stresses on construction materials."

I chuckled. I didn't want to talk shop, either. "What's more official than sitting in one of your favorite architectural elements in the city?"

"I guess you're right. Architecture by proximity?" She smiled and laughed at her own joke.

"I could think of other things that we could do with this proximity. But for the sake of fulfilling my obligation as to this dinner being officially work related, what kind of columns are those?" I gestured up to the tops of the columns that held the small dome above us aloft.

"Are you serious? Corinthian."

"Good. Now that that's settled, we don't have to talk about work at all," I said.

"Then what are we going to talk about?" she asked.

The waiter returned with the wine and to take our order, interrupting my attempt to take this conversation somewhere more interesting. After he took the menus and left, Clarissa leaned forward and asked, "What were you saying?"

I narrowed my gaze as I drank her in. "I think I was going to say something very dangerous about your mouth."

She giggled and licked her lips. "Like how smart it is? Or how I need to keep it shut?"

I hummed. "No. I enjoy listening to you. But you would look pretty with a ball gag."

To my surprise, she didn't blush, but her jaw dropped open. "I... I.." she stammered.

"Joking," I said as I took a sip of wine. "I don't do that kind of stuff. I think the term is 'vanilla' when it comes to my preferences. I like to say my preferences are classic, maybe even old-fashioned."

She closed her mouth and blinked wide-eyed at me. I could see her gulp. "People shouldn't underestimate a good-quality vanilla. It's a strong base for other things."

She spoke slowly and deliberately, carefully choosing her words. We were both very aware that neither of us was talking about a flavor.

The air was charged between us. A crash of lightning caused Clarissa to jump and then laugh, the tension temporarily shattered.

Our dinner was served, and the conversation became very mundane. Was my food good, was hers? Would we be forced to move inside if the storm grew any closer? But my thoughts stayed on her mouth and her plump lips that felt so good to kiss. The tension in my groin had not eased. It only grew more intense as I watched her eat. She slid her lips over her fork with each bite. I had never been so jealous of cutlery.

When the meal was finished and our time in the cupola was over, I stood and held my hand out to Clarissa. Helping her to her feet, I guided her to the edge of the mini temple. There were no guard rails between us and the city from where we stood. Wind whipped toward us, and I held Clarissa closer. Her hair took flight and became a tangled mess. I twisted my fingers in it.

"Sorry it's a mess. The wind." She tried to smooth it down.

"Leave it. I know what you'll look like in the morning with your hair spread over my pillows." I brushed a strand from her face before capturing her chin in my fingers and tilting her face up. "Come home with me," I demanded before claiming her lips.

7

CLARISSA

It was as if my heart had wings and was soaring through the heavens. My nerves danced with ticklish electrical steps up and down my skin. I was surrounded by the dark night sky and twinkling lights. All I could see was Kyle.

He was all there was in my world, his broad, gleaming smile and his pool blue eyes.

I didn't pay attention to our surroundings. I was barely aware that we left the hotel and that we climbed into the back of a car. We arrived at his apartment, but I couldn't have said where we were because all I was aware of was his presence and the way his lips felt against mine.

I knew he was taking me to his home, to his bed. Everything inside his apartment was dark. I didn't pay attention to any of the furnishings because all of my attention was on him, the way his hand wrapped around mine as he led me through rooms. The feel of his skin against mine.

He passed through a door and then stopped and pulled me against his chest. "You can say no if you don't want this," he said.

My hands braced against his broad chest. "What makes you think I don't want this?" I asked.

"I don't want you to think that you're under any obligation simply because of the internship."

I nodded in understanding. "Why are you saying this? I didn't think that at all. It's not, is it?"

A low chuckle rumbled through his chest. "Gods, no. I need to be sure that you're here because you want to be and not for some misplaced sense of obligation."

"I can't think of any place I'd rather be," I admitted.

He lowered his lips to mine. All of my senses were taken up by Kyle. There was the scent of his aftershave, the feel of his bulging muscles under my fingertips, the faint hint of wine on his lips.

Anticipation danced low in my stomach. Kyle slowly undid the buttons of my blouse and pushed the fabric from my shoulders. His lips followed the motion of his fingers, and I shivered at the sensation of his mouth against my neck and my shoulder. Another shudder hitched my breath as his thumb drew lazy circles over the thin fabric of my bra over my nipples.

I gasped and clenched him to me, afraid that if he stopped, if I let go, I would fall, and when I crashed back into reality, it would hurt, and I did not want that. I didn't want reality if this was a dream. I wanted all of the sensations that Kyle's body ignited in my own.

Kyle's eyes looked at me hungrily as he stepped away from me to begin taking his shirt off.

I reached behind me and unhooked my bra, dropping it to the floor beside my feet.

"Clarissa." My name was a low growl in his chest.

It had never sounded so wonderful before. It was as if I had never heard my name said properly in all of my life.

He pulled me back into his arms and lowered me to the cloud-like softness of his bed. I was falling. I knew this wasn't going to hurt because I was falling into Kyle, and he would never hurt me. I knew it in my very soul that he was the man of my dreams and of my future.

I arched against him when he sucked one of my nipples into his mouth. The sensation was more erotic than I ever could have imagined.

"Do you have any idea how beautiful you are?" he murmured against my skin.

His lips left trails of fire across my skin. He made me feel beautiful, made me believe that men did love a full-bodied woman. His fingers bit into my softness as he positioned himself above me.

I moved instinctually, running my leg over his, smoothing my hands over his arms and shoulders.

He reached between us and tickled my folds with the tip of his cock. I gasped as it bumped against the cluster of nerves that was my clit. He moved himself back and forth, playing in the wetness of my desire.

After positioning himself, he pressed his hips forward.

I gasped as he moved into me. It didn't hurt, not the way the books and the movies tried to make it seem. It felt tight as he pushed slowly into me.

"Damn, you are tight," he growled. His breathing sounded labored, but we were both panting from our efforts.

"Is that bad?" I couldn't tell whether he was complaining or not.

"Definitely not. It means this is going to feel really good."

I pushed my heels down against the mattress as I tried to thrust up to meet him hip to hip. It already felt good, even if there was a slight burning sensation as he continued to press in.

He reached between us, and this time, his finger circled my clit. I gasped as rockets shot off inside my body. I don't exactly know what he did to my body, but suddenly, he was able to glide easier.

As he slid back and forth with his cock, and his fingers drew circles against my folds, I was no longer able to focus. It had been hard enough to think before, but all ability was gone. All I knew was Kyle above me, Kyle inside me, and that's all I could have ever hoped and dreamed for.

I cried out as I lost control, and it felt like consciousness wanted to leave my body as spasms of ecstasy overwhelmed me. Kyle clutched me tighter and continued to thrust with increased power and speed.

He roared and pressed hard against me. We were frozen together, all muscles tense and tight. I was still clenching tightly when his body relaxed. It took me a few moments longer to come down from the climax. I would have collapsed against the mattress, but I was already flat on my back. But it did feel like I melted a bit, lost my form as my entire body sighed with a deep, satiated relief. I had never felt so blissfully relaxed.

"I don't think I can move," I admitted.

"Good, I don't want you to go anywhere," Kyle said as he wrapped his arms around me. "Stay with me."

I traced my fingers down the side of his face as I gazed deep into his eyes. They picked up what little light was in the room and winked flashes of bright blue. I stayed with him, and mostly in bed, all of the next day. It was the best weekend ever.

I hated having to leave, but I needed clean clothes and to wear something different to work on Monday morning, not the same outfit everyone saw me leave the office on Friday in. I stayed through dinner, nothing fancy. It was the company that mattered.

My phone pinged with an alert. "My ride will be here in fifteen minutes," I announced.

"Clarissa," Kyle started. "We need to talk."

My insides twisted. "I hope you aren't breaking up with me already," I said with a nervous laugh.

"Hardly, but we should have a little understanding about what is going on here."

I nodded slowly. He was in a position of authority, I knew that. I knew we had to be very careful. "You don't want anyone at the office to know," I said.

"Exactly. I don't want anyone to accuse me of favoritism or improprieties."

I understood what he was saying. Being with Kyle could be disastrous to my internship. But it could also prove to be something wonderful. I wasn't going to be his intern for too much longer. The program ended in about a month, and I would return to my classes. I'd no longer be his intern. We wouldn't have to keep this thing between us a secret.

"I'll see you in the office tomorrow morning," I said. "This is our secret." I leaned in and kissed him.

He held me tight and returned the kiss with a passion that made me want to turn around and let him take me back to bed.

"Yes, secret. Thank you for understanding," he said before kissing me one last time.

I practically floated into the office the next morning, still high from everything Kyle had done to my body over the weekend. I was a ball of dancing nerves as I stepped into his office for our regular Monday morning meeting.

Alayna looked up and smiled at me as she took a sip of coffee.

"Good morning, Clarissa. Did you have a good weekend?" Kyle asked. His smile was holding back his laughter. He knew very well that I had a good weekend.

"As a matter of fact, I did," I answered.

"I went out on the lake and got a sunburn," Steve announced as he walked in behind me.

The bright red stripes across his face with the pale shape of sunglasses announced he'd spent too much time outside without sunscreen.

"Did you get outside at all?" Steve asked.

I shook my head. "I was stuck inside all weekend." I bit my upper lip, refused to look at Kyle, and prayed I wasn't blushing. "But it was totally worth it."

8

KYLE

I reached out and stroked the smooth skin of Clarissa's back. "Where do you think you're going?" I asked.

She sat on the edge of my bed. She twisted and gave me a smile. "I should get dressed. My roommate expects me home at some point during the weekend."

"Will I see you before Monday morning?" I asked.

She shrugged. "Probably not."

I continued to let my fingers play over the expanse of pale skin. "That's not fair," I complained.

"We see each other plenty during the week."

"That's not the same," I pointed out. During the week, we acted as if there was nothing more between us than some flirty banter. As far as I knew, no one at the office was aware of our weekend activities over the past few weeks.

She started to stand up but sat down suddenly and clasped her hands over her face.

"Are you okay?"

She didn't move for a moment and then slowly started to shake her head, but then she stopped moving. She placed one hand out on the mattress to brace herself, and I reached out to her hand, giving her a reassuring squeeze.

"Sorry, I just felt a little wonky there for a second," she said.

I wrapped my arms around her shoulders and pulled her gently back into bed. She didn't resist. "Sounds to me like the universe is telling you that you need to stay in bed." I chuckled.

I smiled as she lay back. I noticed she looked a little green around the edges. "You really don't feel well, do you?"

She whimpered and shook her head slowly. "I think maybe staying in bed and going back to sleep might not be a bad idea." She curled on her side and closed her eyes.

"Do you need me to get you anything?"

She just kept her eyes closed and said no with a low moan.

Concern coursed through my veins like a shot of caffeine. I was suddenly wide awake. Clarissa's face looked pinched and unhappy as she tried to lie still and rest. I tucked the blanket around her and watched over her until I was certain she was asleep. I didn't have any plans other than to be with her and had nothing else to do, so I sat back and turned on the TV to watch a game. I continued to gently stroke her shoulder.

It was several hours before Clarissa woke up. By then, I had gotten dressed and relocated my game watching to the living room. She was dressed and ready to leave when she found me.

"Are you feeling better?" I jumped to my feet and followed her to the front door.

"I still feel a little bit wobbly. There must have been something bad in what I ate last night."

"Are you sure you don't wanna stay here for the rest of the weekend?" I asked.

"I would love nothing more than to spend the rest of the weekend with you. But I haven't seen my roommate in ages, and I promised her we would go to the movies this weekend. It's already Sunday, so I'm running out of time if I'm going to go to a movie with her today."

"As long as you're sure you're feeling okay," I said.

She nodded and gave me a quick kiss and left.

It was the first time in weeks that I had alone time on the weekend. Ever since we got together, we had spent every weekend together. Now, I hardly knew what to do with myself. After another few hours of watching mindless television, I suddenly had a brilliant idea for my client in Hong Kong. I knew not to ignore the Muse when she struck.

I picked up my tablet and began sketching. It was well into the wee hours of the next morning before I realized I hadn't moved. I got up and stretched my stiff muscles and realized that some of my project notes were back at the office.

I decided to change clothes and get dressed for the business day and head into the office. It's not like I hadn't gotten to work early before or pulled all-nighters, so it shouldn't surprise anybody that I came in early to work. Once in the office and with my notes in hand, I returned to sketching.

I lost all track of time until Alayna walked in that morning.

"You got here early," she said, catching my attention.

I looked up to see her standing in my office door. She still had her commute bag slung over her shoulders, and she hadn't yet changed out of her walking shoes.

"Yeah, inspiration struck so I thought I would take advantage of it."

"Strike while the iron is hot," she said. "Are you gonna want some coffee?" she asked.

"That would be a very good idea." I yawned and rubbed my hand over my face. I wasn't a young man anymore, and working around the clock was catching up to me.

"What time did you get in?"

"I can't remember." I yawned again. "But it was dark out, so late."

"Or very early," Alayna pointed out.

She returned a while later with a hot cup of coffee. She set it down on my desk. All of my attention was still on my frantic sketching. She was well aware that sometimes, I got hyper focused on a project until I found the solution.

"Should I handle the kids today?" she asked.

We called the interns 'kids' when it was just the two of us discussing plans. It was probably a little condescending, and it was definitely not politically correct. But they were kids, at least from my age perspective. And I knew Alayna was about the same age as I was. I never asked. It wasn't any of my business, legally. But the interns were young, and they were in the infancy of their architectural careers. It also helped me keep the proper frame of mind when I had to interact with Clarissa whenever she was in the office with me.

"That might not be a bad idea. I'm really on a roll with this. I think the group in Hong Kong is going to be really pleased with the results," I said.

"Are you still thinking about transferring the office there?" Alayna asked.

It had come up before. The client really wanted me on site for the duration of their project, and they were paying me more than enough that being available to them wasn't a bad idea. But I had agreed to and taken on the internship program for the summer, and I had thoughts of settling down with an established office in Chicago.

After Alayna left my office, I sat and contemplated my situation for a few minutes about being in Chicago and about finishing the project in Hong Kong. I loved having an established presence in Chicago. After all, it was the city in the heart of American architecture. But I had that burning drive to see this project completed.

My focus on this project took over my life for a day or two. I went home long enough to shower and change clothes. For the most part, I did a deep intellectual dive into the design and by the end of the week, I was ready to hand over illustrations to my drafting team to see what they could come up with.

"Okay, everybody," I said as I walked into the conference room we used for the interns' office. "I have a new project for you to begin immediately. I really need you to use the drawing and drafting skills you've been showing me that you have."

"What's up?" Steve asked.

He looked eager and excited. When I looked over at Clarissa, she gave me a soft smile but didn't say anything. The corners of her mouth were slightly pinched. I couldn't tell whether she was still not feeling well or she was slightly mad at me for not having said anything to her since she left my apartment on Sunday.

"I've been working on the sketches, and I need them to be turned into presentable drawings. This is not a theoretical exercise. These are for my actual clients, and I just want to see if you can interpret my sketches on something that is going to a client. You've demonstrated skill on the practice runs, let's see how you do when real time and money is involved."

Steve clapped his hands. He was like a kid who just learned they were going to an amusement park. Clarissa looked nervous and nodded repeatedly.

"This is a real client?" she asked nervously.

"Yes, this is a real client Now, whether or not I show them your drawings or I end up sending this over to my draft group will be determined by what you show me by the end of day, tomorrow."

"But this is a real project?" she asked again.

"Yes, this is a real project," I said. "And yes, you can list it on your résumé as part of the work completed during your internship. Alayna has the details and will make sure my sketches are emailed to you. If you have any questions, direct them to her."

"What if we need clarification on something?" Steve asked.

I shook my head. "Ask Alayna. Part of what I want to see from you is how well you translate sketches into a final rendering."

I left Steve chatting excitedly over the project with Alayna. Clarissa seemed quiet. Maybe she was thinking over the task at hand. When I returned to my office, I opened my email and read a new message from the client in Hong Kong. I quickly typed up my response. I didn't have to think about it. I knew what I was going to do.

Planning to arrive in Hong Kong at the end of the month. Looking forward to working with you in person.

9

CLARISSA

I knocked on the open door to Kyle's office. I was already nervous, but when he looked up at me and smiled with those beautiful blue eyes of his, the nerves in my stomach started flipping. It felt like I hadn't seen him for weeks, and honestly, I hadn't. The last time I spent with him was the weekend when I started to feel sick. After that, the internship suddenly was crazy busy, and then the next thing I knew, Steve and I were working on refining Kyle's drawings. We ended up working directly with more senior illustrators to take Kyle's concepts into workable, usable drawings. I had barely seen him at all.

"How are you, Clarissa?" he asked as if he were only my employer and there was nothing going on between us. Maybe there wasn't an *us* anymore.

I glanced over my shoulder before stepping into his office and walking up to his desk. "Are you mad at me?" I blurted out. "We haven't been together for a couple of weeks. You haven't taken me out to dinner. I barely see you."

"I wasn't planning on saying what I was thinking while we were at the office. We had a rule."

"There are questions I can't ask while I stand on this side of your desk in your office," I said.

I watched as realization crossed his face. He dropped his jaw and made an O shape.

"Right," he said, slowly and drawn out. "I'm not mad at you. I'm just very busy. This project has suddenly taken off. It's like an avalanche that we need to keep up with. You understand. My weekends have been taken over completely by this project. I've got a lot to prepare for, and I don't have time for distractions."

I had thought I was more than a distraction for him between big projects. Like a sad puppy, I tucked my proverbial tail between my legs. "Have a good weekend. I hope you get a lot done," I said.

I wasn't able to do much the rest of the day, my focus completely shot. I had completely misread his intentions. I pouted the rest of the day at work and the entire commute home.

I was still pouting and sitting in the dark when Marci came home.

She flicked on the light and jumped before she started giggling nervously. "What the hell are you doing here? Oh, sweetie, why are you sitting here in the dark?"

I slumped to the side, my head resting on the couch and my arms folded in front of me. "I am sitting on the couch in the dark wondering where I went wrong with my life."

Marci sat next to me and patted my hip like she was petting the sad puppy I was. "It's okay, we all go through it."

"You don't understand," I whined.

"I know heartbreak when I see it. I'm sorry," she said.

"How did you get so smart?" I asked as I sat up.

"Wisdom comes with heartache. I've been through more breakups than you have."

"How am I supposed to continue working with him?"

"Well, at least you know your new number-one rule."

I looked at her, waiting to be taught my new rules.

"Never date anyone from work, especially not your boss."

She was right. It was one thing to have a crush on him while I worked for him and something very different to have let him seduce me.

"How am I supposed to survive the next couple of weeks of seeing him every day, knowing that I'm not a priority to him, knowing that I was just something to do before he had something else to occupy his mind?"

"I thought you said you barely see him these days," she said.

She was right. I had barely seen Kyle over the past two weeks, and I no longer shadowed him. I was working with the drafting department. Okay, I could do this. I got to my feet and shuffled over to the tiny kitchen. I opened the fridge and pulled out an energy drink. It was one of the few things I felt like I could actually keep down these days. I had been feeling really woozy for a while.

"Since you're home this weekend, let's get pizza."

The thought of pizza made my stomach grumble, and not in a good 'I'm hungry' way. I set my drink down on the counter, slapped my hand over my mouth, and ran for the bathroom. I didn't know what it was that I had eaten that had my stomach so upset, but this has been going on for a couple of weeks. I rinsed out my mouth and slapped cold water over my face before returning to our tiny living room.

"Are you okay?"

I slowly shook my head. "I've been really woozy lately, and the thought of pizza was too much."

"Oh, God, no." Marci stopped what she was doing, put her hands on her hips, and stared at me. "You're not pregnant, are you?"

"What makes you say that?" Ice cold panic covered my body.

"Well, are you? Have you been using protection?"

My jaw dropped as I tried to remember whether Kyle used condoms. "I think so."

"Oh, shit, Clarissa, you think so?" Marci's tone was laced with concern and judgment.

Oh, shit was right.

We ended up going for a pregnancy test at the drugstore before stopping for Greek food for dinner. I don't know why the thought of lamb smothered in cucumber yogurt sauce didn't make my stomach upset when the thought of cheese pizza made me want to puke. Marci was great and tried to talk about absolutely anything other than the fact that there was a pregnancy test sitting in the shopping bag. All I could focus on was the fact that there was a pregnancy test waiting for me to take it.

"Let's go to a movie tonight," she said.

"Now?" How had she forgotten that I still had to take that test?

"Yes, now. The semester starts in a couple of weeks, and as soon as classes begin, neither of us is going to have time for random movies. It's gonna be study, study, study. You've got your portfolio to develop, and I've got to work on my capstone classes. Senior year is gonna be a real bitch."

I just looked at her, unable to really think about anything. How could I worry about taking capstone classes and building my portfolio when there was a pregnancy test I needed to take and fail? I was terrified. I felt deep in my gut that I was going to pass it with flying colors.

"I don't know, Marci," I said. "I'm just so…"

"I know you're preoccupied. Why do you think I'm trying to take your mind off it? Come on, you can pee on that stick in the morning just as easily as you can tonight. I'll buy popcorn."

I gave in and we went to the movies. I spent the entire movie wondering if the characters up on the screen were as dumb as me. Did they use protection? Of course, they did. None of them were pregnant, or were they? The action and comedy on screen couldn't take my mind away from being preoccupied over the pregnancy test.

For Marci's sake, I pretended that I was paying attention. I pretended to eat a handful of popcorn when I could barely choke down one kernel at a time

Back in the apartment, I let Marci take the bathroom first and get ready for bed before I went in there. I stared at the instructions, knowing what they were telling me, but I still stared at them as if I could find out whether I was pregnant or not by reading them. I watched as the purple lines slowly showed up. Definitely purple lines, and they grew darker, two of them. There shouldn't have been two of them. I didn't want to be pregnant. I didn't want to accept the truth.

"Are you okay in there?"

I didn't say anything.

"Clarissa, it's gonna be okay," Marci said softly through the door.

"No, it's not." I opened the door and continued to stand in front of the sink and stare down at the positive test.

She wrapped her arms around my shoulders. "We'll figure this out. You're not alone."

"What am I supposed to tell him? He has barely spoken to me. When I asked if I was gonna get to see him this weekend, he told me he was really busy."

I spent the rest of my weekend trying to figure out exactly how I was going to tell Kyle he was going to be a father. I took long walks and I practiced my words. There had to be a better way to get the words that I needed without feeling like an idiot.

Monday came around, and I was so nervous. I couldn't have eaten even if my stomach was behaving and letting me keep anything down. I planned on immediately going to Kyle and getting this over with. Why drag it out? Why torture myself? But as soon as I got to the office, Alayna had me and Steve leave with her to an offsite facility that would take Kyle's drawings and build models.

Every time I went to go see Kyle, Alayna had another project for me to work on and managed to send me in a different direction so that I didn't see him. I knew he had a busy week, that he had meetings with his client. But I also wanted to let him know what was going on.

I hated the fact that when I finally did manage to get to his office on Friday, he was already gone for the day.

I didn't bother to try to find him the following week. It was the last week of the internship. I had to see him. I went to his office. The door was locked and the lights were off.

"Can I help you with something?" Alayna asked.

"I was looking for Kyle," I said.

"Well, he's not here."

"I noticed. Do you know when he's getting back? I wanted to tell him something."

"He flew to Hong Kong."

"Hong Kong?" I could barely fathom what she was saying.

"Didn't he mention that to you? I guess he was too busy. What did you want to tell him? Maybe I could pass it along for you?"

"I wanted to thank him for the internship," I said, trying to think of something to say that wasn't blurting out the way I'd let him knock me up. "I wanted to tell him personally. Do you know when he'll be back?"

"He's not planning on coming back for a while. He bought a one-way ticket."

10

KYLE

I gave myself plenty of time to get to Hong Kong. International travel always kicked my butt. It took too much time, too much effort, and for the amount of actual effort that was involved, I spent most of my time sitting on my ass or asleep in an airplane.

It was still exhausting having an open-ended travel schedule. I still had to hustle through airports and make connections. But it was nice not to have to stress over the hustle to get to the hotel where I would have to scramble to make it to appointments and meetings while feeling like a zombie while pretending I was anything but, only to have to repeat the process to go home, all in less than a week's time. It was nice to be able to relax through the process.

Airports would always be airports, and that part of traveling always took a certain level of energy. But for once, it was great that as soon as I landed in Hong Kong, I wasn't in a huge hurry to get everything together for a meeting. I had given myself more than a couple of days to allow myself to get settled, get over the jet lag, and catch up on sleep.

One of the first things I did as soon as I arrived was to plan with Alayna to have the building models shipped directly to the client. As soon as she was able to give me an estimated arrival schedule, I called and made meeting arrangements with the client.

I may not have had to be in the client's office right away, but it didn't mean I wasn't busy. During the few days of downtime, I located an apartment and signed a one-year lease. I also was able to spend time surveying the job site on my own. I wanted to take a look without having to answer any questions or provide any opinions. I had seen copious photos and videos of the location, but that was never quite the same as being there in person. Photos and videos always miss something. I liked to see the whole picture, not just the pit where the foundation was being constructed, or the buildings next to the site. I liked to see the entire neighborhood, and yes, tall office buildings had neighborhoods. Even a working community was a community.

I wanted to see what I was working with before I jumped into all of the work.

The design was mostly done. My job moving forward was to make the necessary modifications that would inevitably come up as construction met the obstacles of permits and environmental special interest groups.

I was in constant contact with Alayna in Chicago. At this point, I planned on returning after several months. I had a year lease because finding anything less than that was next to impossible. I had no intention of staying if the project wrapped up and was completed within that time. I was only able to work in Hong Kong because my office was based in the States, and I was only serving as a consultant for my client. I relied on her to keep my Chicago presence ongoing.

She even wrapped up all the necessary paperwork for the internship program. She wrote extensive reviews on each intern and provided letters of recommendation under my name. Overall, I considered the program a success. It felt good to give back to the architectural education community, even if I had mentally checked out on the last several weeks. By then, all the interns were wrapping up their projects and getting ready to start their next semester's classes.

I received a smattering of emails from the group. Bella and Kendall must have used the same template since they were practically identical, except for the signatures at the end. Conner straight out asked me for a job. The other Steve's note was similar to the one sent by the girls, formulaic. Sick Steve's message was the most honest one of the group. He pointed out his favorite things that he had the opportunity to complete and work on over the summer. He was really the only one I would consider doing a portfolio review for once he graduated. Him and Clarissa. Only I didn't hear from her. There was no message from Clarissa.

A small pang of guilt flared in my chest over how I left things with Clarissa. I realized I left without saying goodbye. That was a dick move. This was a business decision. She had to understand. What we had together had been fun, but my career was my priority, just as I knew hers was for her. She was a talented woman. She would go far.

I lost myself in the work and the hectic life of living in a city like Hong Kong. Chicago had a certain energy to it, and I would never call it laid back. But the energy in Hong Kong was so much more frenetic. I didn't have time to think about past mistakes, and I didn't even think about Clarissa at all. Not until I was leaving work one day a few months after I had settled in. It was one of those cold, blustery days.

Hong Kong is an international city, but someone shaped like Clarissa and with her coloring would still stand out. It was the hair, flying in the wind, that first caught my attention. There simply weren't that many blondes with Clarissa's curves. I saw her walking away from me with that hip sway of hers that was hard to forget. My breath caught in my throat. I changed my direction and turned to follow her. After about half a block, I was about to call out her name. I would say how amazed I was to see her, what a coincidence to run into her on the streets of Hong Kong, of all places. And then she stopped. She turned and said something to her companion.

She wasn't Clarissa. I stopped in my tracks and just stared at her for a while. I couldn't tell whether I was disappointed or relieved. I thought about Clarissa often for the next couple of days before work took over and all of my focus was back on the building.

"When are you coming back?" Alayna asked.

I had already been in Hong Kong for over six months. The building seemed to be taking forever.

"I'm here for at least another five months. We keep running into hiccups with the building commissions," I said.

"Sounds like someone hasn't been paying their bribes," she joked.

"Maybe not." I chuckled. "It's not like that anymore. Mostly ecological reasons. I've been thinking…" I paused.

"Don't tell me, you want me out there?" she asked.

"Damn, you are always one step ahead of me," I admitted. "I think now is the time to set up an international office."

"We need to discuss who will run the Chicago office if I'm in Hong Kong," Alayna pointed out. "I'm not going to be the person flying halfway around the world, back and forth every other week."

"I think I might want to shut Chicago down for now. Get a local office going here, and then expand back into the States. Come here for a couple of weeks. We'll get into it, really dig in deep for what needs to take place—keep that office up and running, or move everyone here."

"Kyle, you always dream and plan big," she said.

"How do you think I got to be where I am?"

I began the process of what it would take to immigrate and get a proper work visa so that I could take on other clients while I stayed here. Chicago would always have a special place in my heart, but I was where I needed to be.

Around the time I started discussing setting up a local firm, I received an email from Sick Steve—I was probably going to think of him with that nickname for the rest of my life.

'I wanted to thank you for the great letter of recommendation. I know Alayna wrote it and signed for you. I've also sent her a thank you. I've been accepted into an accelerated graduate program. I will be done with my studies this time next year and was just wondering if you would consider having an opening for me? I would love to work with you again sometime, in any capacity.'

I didn't even think about my response. Steve would make a great addition to any team.

'I'd be glad to review your portfolio once you are done with your studies. One thing you need to understand, though, is that I'm setting up new offices in Hong Kong, and you'd have to be willing to come out here.'

I hit *Send*. A sudden thought of Clarissa hit me. What was she up to? She should be graduating soon. Where was she going for her master's studies? In all this time, she hadn't reached out to me once. Had she followed up with Alayna at all?

I shook my head and cleared her out. I had a building to see through to the final construction and an office to establish. I didn't have time for thinking about mistakes that had been made and wondering what a woman I once knew was doing half a world away.

11

CLARISSA

Six years later

"Night, Boss," I said as I shut down my computer and turned the lamp over my desk off. I grabbed my water bottle and my tote bag before I headed out the door.

"Night, Clarissa. Do you have class tonight?"

"No, I'm just picking up Leo. We're gonna have a quiet night at home. I've got to study, so I'm sure that means Leo will learn everything he didn't want to know about Roman concrete." I had a habit of reading the more interesting things I was learning out loud.

"I'm sure he'll find Roman concrete fascinating," James Stone, my boss, said.

"We'll see," I started. "Sometimes, he thinks what I'm learning is interesting. Most of the time, that's not nearly as fascinating as the little creatures in his video games. I have to go before I'm late picking him up from daycare. I'll see you in the morning."

I hiked my bag onto my shoulder and headed out. I took the elevated train out to our neighborhood and walked a few blocks to the daycare.

"Mommy!" Leo shouted as soon as I stepped in the door. He already had his coat on, and his bag was sitting there waiting next to the door.

"Am I late?" I asked as I noticed he and the other child were more than ready.

"No, you're fine. Leo and Joey are the only two left, so I figured it would be easier to have them ready to go," Miss Franny, the teacher for his daycare class, said.

I scooped Leo up and held them on my hip.

"How was kindergarten today?" I asked.

"I learned how to read. I can read, Mommy," he said.

I looked over at Franny.

"Apparently, they're starting sight words in his class. He's been reading all afternoon long."

"That's fantastic," I said.

"He's reading words that he shouldn't already know. I mean, he's actually reading and not just pretending to know what the words say. You've got a smart one there," Franny said.

I tickled and kissed Leo on the cheek. "I knew you were a smart boy."

I still held him on my hip as I signed him out, then set him down and helped him with his backpack. I took his hand, and we walked the few blocks from the school to our apartment.

Leo held my hand and skipped along as we walked home. He pointed out every sign that he could read. "Mommy, that says 'Stop'. Mommy, that sign says 'Shoe'."

And then he pointed at the yellow awning across the street. "That says 'Pizza'. Can we have pizza for dinner?"

I stared down at him. He really was reading. Not once had he pointed at the yellow awning with the big red letters and announced that it said 'pizza' before. I was impressed.

"Since you can read that sign, I think you deserve pizza for dinner."

We walked up to the corner and waited for the light before crossing the street. I knew plenty of other people who would've just waited for traffic and then dashed across. But I was trying to teach Leo proper pedestrian rules and that if he needed to cross the street, he needed to look both ways and go to a corner and wait for the light to tell him to cross.

Once inside the pizzeria, I asked if he recognized any other words when I pointed up to the menu. The menu was a series of large whiteboards covered in letters with all of the different choices and all of the different sizes and all of the different prices.

Leo's blue eyes went wide, and he shook his head, a little panicked. It could be overwhelming when you could read.

I ordered a medium pizza with his favorite things on half and my favorite things on the other half. The warm, savory smell of pizza filled our small, cozy apartment. Leo couldn't put his school bag in his room fast enough or wash his hands and face fast enough. He was eager to dig in.

Just as predicted, I spent the evening studying ancient Roman construction methods. Specifically, concrete. Specifically, the recent rediscovery on why Roman concrete was as brilliant a building material as it was. Not only did it seem to withstand the test of time, but it also self-healed whenever cracks formed. For close to two thousand years, modern builders had been struggling to find out what the secret was. It turned out it was something fairly simple. It came down to hot salt water. And the weirdest thing about that was it took a chemist from MIT to "rediscover" that fact.

Our morning routine was fairly simple. I woke up first and gave Leo a pre-wake-up kiss. He woke up slowly, so I did my best to give him plenty of time and not try to rush him while he was struggling to face the day. Once out of the shower, I made sure he was out of bed and in the bathroom. He was old enough to potty and brush his teeth without me hovering over him. He still needed verbal prompting, but I could yell my instructions from my room while I got dressed.

I helped him to pick out his clothes for the day, and while he got dressed—again, this was something he was old enough to do on his own—I made our lunches for the day. Any grogginess left in our systems was chased out by a brisk walk to the school.

"Love you," I said as he ran into the school yard. I had been allowed to kiss him goodbye for exactly two days, and then he announced that only babies got kisses. He let me kiss him when I picked him up. I think whichever kid it was who picked on him about my kissing him wasn't around in the afternoons. It squeezed my heart that my little boy was growing up.

It wasn't a full two blocks to the train, and then another short walk and I was back in the office. I was set up at my desk in the front and had coffee brewing before anyone else got in.

"Clarissa, could you join me in my office?" James asked as I walked in the door.

"Right now?" I asked, getting to my feet.

"Please."

I followed him to the back of the firm's offices, stopping long enough to pour his morning cup of coffee.

"What's up?" I asked as I placed the cup of coffee on his desk.

"You know my plan is to eventually sell the firm?" James asked.

I nodded. In my dreams, I would graduate with my master's and somehow suddenly have enough money to buy the firm from him.

But I knew I was years and years away from being in a position to have my own firm, and James was much closer to retirement for that to ever happen for me.

"It looks like I may have lined someone up."

"But I didn't think you were ready to retire for another few years?" I said. I tried to hide the panic in my voice. James couldn't sell already. I wasn't ready yet.

"I didn't expect to. But an opportunity has come up, and if I can take an early retirement…" He let out a long breath. "My wife would murder me in my sleep if she found out I passed up a golden opportunity to retire early. She's ready to move up to Minneapolis to be close to the grandkids without me."

I bit my upper lip and nodded. He was my boss. He didn't owe me anything. We had talked extensively about my plans once I had my degree, and he had offered to help launch my career. But in the end, that was just talk. No promises had been made, and no contracts had been signed. I tried to hide my disappointment behind a weak smile.

"I'll still be around, and I know how to use a phone. I said I would help mentor, and I plan on following through. Just because I might retire a little sooner than planned, it doesn't mean my contacts are going away."

I nodded some more. His words felt like empty promises. He would retire and move up to lake country and forget all about helping the young architectural student who had spent the last three years answering phones for his company. I blinked and prayed that he didn't notice I was trying hard not to cry. The past few years had been hard. I finally felt like I was making progress, and this was a blow to my plans.

I cleared my throat. "Who are you talking to about this? Is it a firm I know?" I asked.

"Probably. The guy has been out of the country for a few years. My understanding is he is trying to reestablish a presence in the Chicago area. You've heard of Kyle Love, right?"

My eyes went wide. Kyle was back. I hadn't heard his name in years, not since I was a hapless intern for him and let him seduce me before abandoning me and his growing firm to relocate to Hong Kong. I didn't want anything to do with him. I didn't even include that I had interned for him the summer before I dropped out of school for a few years.

"Yeah, I have heard of him. I didn't realize he was in the States."

Kyle was back, and I was going to see him. Damn it. I thought about him every day, even though I didn't want to. It was hard not to when his son had the same pool blue eyes.

12

KYLE

It was good to be back in the States. It was good to be back in Chicago. The way Hong Kong changed every few months, I had almost expected Chicago to look completely different. All the time I was gone, it was almost as if the city was put on pause. I felt like everything was the same. I knew it wasn't, but there was a certain energy here, and that hadn't changed at all.

I felt Hong Kong was constant and pushing toward the future, while Chicago felt established and like the strong foundations of a building that would launch forward. Chicago wasn't chasing after anything because eventually, everything would come to it.

I successfully managed to convince Alayna to come work for me in Hong Kong. She had agreed to only stay a couple of years. I wasn't allowed to make her move around the world and expect her to stay forever. The second I mentioned thinking about moving back to the States, she began pushing for it. I didn't think she particularly liked living abroad. It was an adventure that some people didn't take to.

Alayna was invaluable to my company, and I didn't think I could do my job without her supporting me. I could let her quit, but I didn't want the struggle of finding another assistant.

"I've worked remotely before. I can do it again," she reminded me. And then she booked herself a return flight. She came back a good three months before I even booked a plane ticket, but she still worked for me. Even from half a globe away, she still did an absolute amazing job of anticipating my every need. And that included scoping out architectural firms that might be interested in partnerships or selling.

I wasn't surprised in the least that I had an appointment with the Stone Group within a few weeks of returning home. The Stone Group's offices were close to where my last Chicago office had been located, so I knew the neighborhood. It had cleaned up a little bit. There had been some rehabilitation construction previously, but that was all done now. There were good restaurants, and it was conveniently located near pretty much anywhere in the city.

There was something very familiar about walking into the Stone Group's offices. I don't know if it was the way the receptionist smiled at me or even the building itself. There was something that seemed comforting about being there, like I belonged.

I stepped up to the receptionist desk, and she blinked at me a few times. She was quite lovely. "You must be Kyle Love to see James Stone," she said.

I didn't even need to introduce myself. Maybe she seemed so familiar because she was smart and anticipated my next moves much like Alayna did.

"I am. I believe he is expecting me," I said.

"I will show you to the conference room." As she stood up, an older gentleman stepped in the lobby and introduced himself.

"Mr. Love? James Stone."

He held out his hand. His grip was firm, and I could tell that he had a history that included the actual construction of buildings and was not limited to only designing them.

"Come on back," he said.

The receptionist returned to her seat, and I followed James. He asked me perfunctory pre-meeting types of questions as we strolled through the office. Was I acclimatizing back to life in Chicago after having lived abroad? Did I want something to drink, water, coffee? And other pleasantries that didn't mean very much.

He led me into a large conference room, and we took the two seats at the head of the table. It was just the two of us, and while it seemed like excess in this room, I understood we were more on equal footing here than if we had gone into his office and I sat across his desk from him like I was at some kind of awkward job interview. I guess this was a job interview of sorts. He wanted to know if I was the right kind of architect and the right kind of boss to take over his company. After all, if I bought him out, I wasn't simply handing him money for the purpose of using his office. I was taking on his employees and his clients. He needed to know whether he could trust me with all of them, but I was also interviewing him.

I needed to know if his employees and his clients were good enough for me. After all, I had a reputation to uphold, a certain level of design standard I expected to be allowed to do. I wasn't in this business to redecorate Mid-Century kitchens or to create aesthetically pleasing additions onto houses that were built over a century ago. That's not the kind of work I did.

I shouldn't have been worried. Alayna wouldn't have set up a meeting with somebody who was in the business of house remodels when I was in the business of skyscrapers.

We ended up talking for several hours. At some point, his pretty receptionist brought in a deli order of subs, and we continued to talk. I tried not to stare at her while she was setting up our lunches, but I knew I knew her from somewhere. I just couldn't put my finger on it. I expected that I would feel very foolish once I realized who she was.

The entire setup sounded to me to be a great fit. And he would be a great asset. I wished I had met him a few years earlier. He was the kind of person I would have liked to work with during my career. It was almost sad that I was only just now getting to know him.

Stone had a small, dedicated group that I felt would fit nicely in with the aesthetic of my design group. I would be integrating my current design group with his and taking on his existing client list. The type of work they specialized in was a good fit.

"I think it's safe to say this was a very informative meeting," I said as we wrapped things up.

"What are your thoughts on continuing this conversation?" Stone asked.

It wasn't an unreasonable question, especially since this had been our initial meeting to see if business-wise, this would be a compatible transaction.

I chuckled. "I don't know about you, but I originally had this down on my schedule for an hour. I've been here closer to three. To be honest, right now, this feels like a fit. I absolutely think we need to continue this conversation."

"That's what I like to hear. Have your assistant reach out, and we'll get something on the books for next week."

He walked me out after our meeting, and we shook hands again. I was impressed with the strength that he still held in his body. I could only hope that I would still be that fit when I reached his age.

As I said goodbye one more time, I caught a glimpse of something the receptionist did and suddenly, my mind was flooded by memories. My body instantly reacted. I had the smells of fruit and roses in my nose and the sensation of wind whipping around me as a storm rolled in.

"Clarissa, is that you?" I asked.

She looked up and bit her upper lip the way I remember she would. But this time, she wasn't blushing. She nodded. "I didn't think you recognized me, so I wasn't going to say anything."

"You should've said something. I didn't recognize you. You've changed your hair."

She reached up and touched her hair behind her ear. She had it in a bun style, and as far as I could recall, I had only ever seen her wear it cascading over her shoulders. How had I missed recognizing her? Had a simple hairstyle really changed everything about her?

"How long has it been? A couple of years, right?"

"Closer to six," she said.

"You know each other?" James asked. He was still standing next to her desk.

"I spent a summer interning at his offices a while ago," she admitted.

"I don't remember your saying anything about it," he said.

"It's been a long time, and it was before I graduated. I don't really include much on my résumé from more than five years ago. And I was a student," she continued to explain.

I couldn't stop staring at her. She no longer looked like the young college girl I remembered. Her lips were just as plump and kissable as I remembered, but there was a certain set to her mouth she didn't have before.

"We should go out and get coffee sometime. You know, catch up."

She smiled and nodded. She cast a quick glance over at her boss.

"There's nothing much to catch up on. I understand you've been in Asia. Singapore?"

"I've been in Hong Kong. And you've been in Chicago this whole time?"

"Of course. Where else would I go?" She glanced down when her phone started to ring. "If you'll excuse me, Jenna is paging me. I'll be right back." She scurried out from behind her desk.

This time, I took a good look at her. She still had the same delicious curves, and she walked with a wiggle in her hips that did things to the blood supply in my brain. But she was dressed like a middle-aged librarian. That had to be why I didn't recognize her. The Clarissa from the internship had been borderline quiet, almost shy, but she had a sense of style that spoke volumes. She hadn't seemed to care about societal norms and wore combat boots with dresses.

Stone caught me staring.

"I'm surprised to see her here. But I was mostly surprised I didn't recognize her right away. Is she as smart as I remember?"

13

CLARISSA

Panic flooded my system. I couldn't believe I was staring at Kyle Love. Damn, he looked good. His eyes were the same beautiful clear blue. I couldn't forget them, even if I wanted to. He looked a little older, more rugged. His hair was a little longer, and there was creasing next to his eyes. It suited him.

He was even more handsome than the man I had fallen in love with so many years ago. It took every ounce of self-restraint I clutched onto to not burst into tears and become hysterical. I couldn't react the way my gut wanted me to react.

I wanted to yell and scream. I wanted to laugh. I had to fight the urge to throw things at him while at the same time, I needed to launch myself over the desk and into his arms and pepper his face with kisses. I wanted to forgive him for having abandoned me.

How was it possible to have so many emotions all at once? I wanted to strangle him for not even telling me he was leaving the country. I was nothing more than confused emotions and anger and joy all wrapped up in a skin suit.

I bit down every single conflicting emotion that fought to take hold and smiled at the man.

"You're Kyle Love and you're here to see James," I managed to say.

He smiled, the little lines crinkling at his eyes. His brows drew together ever so slightly. I could tell he was trying to remember my name. That was a blow to my already fragile sanity that barely hung by a thread.

I needed to get rid of Kyle, and get rid of him fast, so that I could lock myself in the bathroom and hyperventilate or maybe throw up. Fortunately, James unknowingly rescued me.

In his excitement to meet and discuss selling the business to Kyle, James was by my desk before I could press the intercom. If a sixty-five-year-old man could look like an excited puppy, it was James. They introduced themselves and shook hands and went off to the conference room. I was spared the indignity of having to walk next to Kyle Love and pretend that I was okay with it.

I left my desk and went to the office manager's office.

"Hey, Jenna," I said. "I need to step out. Can you watch the front?"

"Of course. Are you getting coffee?"

"I might." I didn't know what I was going to do. I just needed to leave.

"Will you bring me something back?" She didn't need to give me her order. I knew exactly what she wanted. She ordered the same thing every time, a large, iced mocha double-pump vanilla.

Of course, I didn't think walking down the block to the coffee shop was going to be enough to ease the boiling in my mind and my gut. Kyle Love walked into my job, and he didn't recognize me.

I focused on that for a few moments too many. He didn't recognize me.

Maybe it was just as well. I could go about my life. He could go about his. And I never would have to tell him about Leo. That was a conversation I didn't know whether I could have. It had been hard enough to try to tell him when I first found out I was pregnant. And even though that conversation never occurred, I still fought through the stress and the tears to prepare myself to tell him. How was I supposed to tell him now, all this time later?

As if on autopilot, I found myself walking into the coffee shop and ordering. My stomach still wanted to twist in on itself by the time I got back to the office with Jenna's coffee and another one for myself.

"Are they going to want lunch?" I asked Jenna before crossing from her office to look in the conference room through the large glass wall.

James and Kyle were intently discussing something. They both had those little smiles on their faces. I remembered that expression on Kyle's face when he became manic about an idea. James always had a similar expression when he got really into a project. He didn't display the same level of obsessive intensity that Kyle did. Seeing them together like that, it was obvious they were definitely excited about what they were discussing.

"I should go ahead and just order them lunch," I said, returning to Jenna's office.

"That's not a bad idea," she said. "I know what James would get, but I haven't a clue what the other guy would eat," she admitted.

"Oh, don't worry about that. I'll give his assistant a call and find out." I didn't need to call Alayna to find out what Kyle wanted. He was a classic club sandwich guy. He always commented something whenever sandwiches had been brought in. I stopped and shook my head. Funny how I remembered what he liked to eat, and weird that I just assumed Alayna would still be working for him.

"While I'm at it, do you want me to order you anything?" I asked.

"I would kill for a turkey with avocado," Jenna said.

"I can do that."

"Are you gonna order something for yourself?"

I shrugged. "I'm tempted to order everybody lunch."

If James was in a good mood, he'd pay for everyone's food. And from the look I saw on his face, it was a safe bet that he was in a good mood. I headed into the back to get Phillip's and Michelle's orders. If I was gonna order delivery for two, I might as well order delivery for six.

I spent the rest of my day anticipating having to talk to Kyle again. Just the thought of having to say 'Goodbye' or 'Have a nice day' was eating me up inside. How was I going to face him on a daily basis if he's the one who took over?

I was almost through with my master's program, and I was going to have to start my final internship soon. It had simply been too long and drawn out of a process to finish my education that my time in Kyle's office all those years ago barely counted anymore.

I had options. I didn't have to keep working for the Stone Group. I could get another job in Chicago, at least through graduation, and then I could leave if I wanted to.

It wasn't as if there weren't other architectural firms. Just because Kyle Love was back in Chicago, that didn't mean that our paths had to cross again. After all, Chicago was a pretty big city. It was huge, and if he could leave the country to work, there was no reason I couldn't leave the state.

There were other places in this country that I could go. I had always thought about moving to the Pacific Northwest, Portland or Seattle. They always looked like fun, interesting places. Or maybe I'd even go south to Atlanta. There were places I would be able to get a job. I didn't have to stay here. I didn't have to stay where Kyle Love was, especially if he didn't remember me.

I needed to calm down. This was just an introductory meeting. It wasn't as if he were actually gonna buy out James Stone.

My stomach and my nerves were a mess the rest of the day. They didn't settle down until after Kyle actually had recognized me and he left the office. That had been minutes of torture. I might have hated it that he hadn't recognized me, but having to pretend to be nice to his face after he figured out who I was… it sucked.

I wasn't sure how I felt about it, either. Didn't it just prove that I hadn't been important to him? After all, he managed to leave me without even saying goodbye. And when he came back, he didn't recognize me right away.

I had accepted what the reality was a long time ago. Kyle Love changed everything about my life. He would always be more important to me and have a greater impact on me than he would ever know. It didn't matter that he could walk back into my life, smile the way he smiled, and my toes would curl. None of that mattered because he made it very clear that I was not a priority to him.

I remembered everything I had tried to forget over the past six years. And I remembered all of the little moments since that were so important to me, that I thought should have been so important to him. And that he would never know about what he had missed. There was no way I would tell Kyle now about his son. I couldn't for my own sanity, and not for Leo's. I had to keep my little boy safe.

I left work early. The train didn't go fast enough, and I practically ran all the way to the school to pick Leo up. He was happy to see me, but maybe not as happy as I was to see him. I hugged him tight until he squirmed.

"You're squishing me," he complained.

"I missed you today," I said. I rubbed my face against his dark hair, mostly so he wouldn't see that I had tears in my eyes. "What do you want for dinner tonight?" I asked.

I decided I would buy him whatever he wanted. Leo didn't need to know anything about his father. Or that I was feeling guilty over the entire situation, and that a special dinner was my silent way of saying I was sorry for this whole mess.

14

KYLE

My mind raced with the possibilities of taking over for James Stone.

"Alayna," I called out from my desk in the small office space I currently occupied.

She walked into my office, her eyebrows lifted to her hairline in question.

"What if we didn't sign the lease for the space on West Madison?"

"This place is big enough. As it is, your top designers are working from their kitchen tables. I know they would like proper drafting tables to work at because Nick has already complained about it. You are going to need to set up an office somewhere." She spoke as if I were a child not understanding her words.

"I was thinking, what if we held out for the Stone Group and moved in with them?"

"I thought that was just an initial talk. How fast is he willing to sell?" she asked.

I shrugged. I wasn't certain, but they had a good space, and I didn't see any reason to move the setup they had when I didn't even have a proper office ready.

"I guess we could hold off signing the lease until we know whether your agreement with Stone Group will go through. But there's no guarantee the property will still be available at that point. Are their offices really that much better?"

"The interior decoration is fabulous. Good energy flows in the floor plan. Really good location. It's only a couple of blocks from West Madison," I said. I had been thinking about the space for hours. I could easily work there.

"Is it large enough? We're bringing in how many employees?" she asked. I could always trust Alayna to be pragmatical.

"It's a small firm with only ten employees," I said.

"And we'll bring in another six or so. You need space for at least twenty people. Is their space big enough? Can we easily expand it?"

"Hmm." I thought about what she was saying. The office building he was in potentially could be expanded into, but I didn't know the occupancy in the rest of the property. I hadn't exactly looked at it from that perspective. "That's something you can look into, right?"

Alayna nodded. She was the best assistant a guy could have.

"Why didn't you tell me his assistant was Clarissa?" I asked before she had a chance to leave.

Alayna paused and stared at me. "Pardon?"

"Clarissa, do you remember her? She was one of the interns with Steve," I said.

"Yes, I remember Clarissa. I didn't know she was James Stone's assistant."

"I thought you set up the meeting with her," I said.

"I believe the woman I spoke with was named Jenna. Was Clarissa there?"

"She was. Maybe she's just the receptionist. I must have assumed she was his assistant because she had always struck me as being more ambitious than wanting to be somebody's receptionist." What had happened to her? How had she gone from a talented architectural student with potential to a receptionist who answered phones?

"Can you set up another meeting for us?" I asked Alayna before she stepped out of my office.

"Of course. Do you have a preference for date and time?"

"Let's give it a week. I don't want him to think I'm too enthusiastic," I said with a chuckle. I was pretty sure James Stone already knew I was eager for this deal.

The following week, when I walked into the Stone Group's offices, Clarissa was perched behind the receptionist desk.

"Hello, Clarissa, nice to see you again," I said, genuinely pleased to see her.

"Kyle." She smiled, but it didn't seem genuine. More like she was pretending because she had to greet me as I walked in the door. "James is expecting you. I'll let him know that you're here."

I leaned against her desk and hovered as she pushed buttons on her phone and told her boss that I was waiting. She hung up and looked back up at me.

"He said he'll be right out. Why don't you have a seat?" She gestured toward the overstuffed chairs situated in the lobby area. They looked like they had never been sat in.

"I'm okay right here," I said. I continued to lean on the receptionist desk.

"I really can't believe how good it is to see you again."

"Thank you. It's been a few years. How did you like Hong Kong? Were you there the entire time?"

"Hong Kong was great. I had a consulting contract onsite for a client, and then I decided to stay and expand my client base," I told her.

"What brought you back to Chicago?" she asked.

"Chicago has always felt like I belong here, and I had unfinished business. So I wanted to come back. Do you still like those little secret temples on top of buildings?" I asked, remembering that she liked those little hidden gems in the architecture of Chicago.

"I still like those. I can't believe you remembered that," she said. "It's been a while."

"I remember quite a few things," I admitted, thinking about how it felt to kiss her and how her body felt in my bed. "You should go out to dinner with me," I said.

She leaned forward conspiratorially. "Why would I do that?" Her eyes seemed to almost gleam wickedly.

"Because I seem to recall we got along very well," I said as I raised my brows in a knowing waggle.

She leaned away from me. This time, there was a slight tinge of blush on her cheeks. "We did, didn't we?"

"See, you should go out to dinner with me."

"I don't think that would be a good idea." She shot my invitation down.

Before I had a chance to say anything else, James stepped out and asked if I was ready to go. He gestured for me to lead the way out the door.

"Are you stepping out for lunch? When should I expect you back if you have any calls?" Clarissa asked.

"We should be back in the next two to three hours," James said as we left.

Lunch was only two and a half hours long, surprisingly enough. We skipped the chit-chat and got into some of the more in-depth details that purchasing his architectural firm would entail.

"If you were to do a complete buyout, what would you see my role as in this process?" James asked.

"If we are talking about a complete buyout," I started, "Your role would be that of a wealthy, retired architect. However, you had mentioned the potential for a takeover process, in which case I would take ownership over the course of a couple of years. If we were to follow that line of thinking, I would see you as a senior consultant. We would discuss what percentage of time I could rely on your expertise, and with each year, that percentage diminishing until you were fully retired. How does that sound?"

"I do like the sound of wealthy retired architect. However, I have to admit the thought of handing all of my clients over for me to just go and sit by the side of the lake with my grandkids is a little daunting. I want my clients to be confident in my choice as well," he said.

"I think your clients would be more comfortable if you were around in a consulting role for a year or two. I don't think this is something that we would need to drag out. Watch, you'll get used to being retired real quick, and you'll want to shrink those consultation hours down to nothing within a few months."

I was ready to sign a check and take over, but I did like the thought of having James around for six months to a year to really see how he intellectually translated client needs from initial ideas through drawn concepts and into constructed buildings.

"I think we need to work out some details and maybe get some lawyers involved at this point," he said.

I couldn't agree more. We continued to chat about some of the minor details as we walked back to his office. I had questions about how easy the property management company at the current location was to work with and admitted that I was interested in maintaining the same space.

I followed him inside but stayed in the lobby. I wanted to catch a few minutes with Clarissa alone. She wasn't there, so I said my goodbyes to James and waited.

"Oh, you're here," she said as she turned the corner from the back of the office. "Do you need me to call James for you?"

"No, I wanted to see you," I admitted.

She raised her brows and waited for me to continue.

"If you won't have dinner with me to catch up on old times, would you come have dinner with me so that I can pick your brain about the Stone Group?" I asked.

"I am not going to give away any business secrets," she said.

I chuckled. "That's not exactly the kind of information I'm looking for. I'm more interested in…"

"I know what it's for. You're looking at purchasing the business. I guess I could do that." She bit her lip, which I knew meant she was thinking. "I can meet you for dinner on Friday night."

"Friday night it is. Should I make reservations?" I asked.

"Do you mind if I pick?" she asked.

I gave her my phone number and told her to text me where she wanted me to meet her.

15

CLARISSA

I couldn't believe I agreed to have dinner with Kyle. What was I thinking? Clearly, I wasn't. But I had been smart enough to have him give me a couple of days to arrange for a babysitter. Even though he did not know that was the delay.

I held my breath as I sent Kyle a message that I would meet him at this little Italian place. He'd have no problems finding it. It was a family friendly restaurant, bright lights, no secluded tables. Nothing vaguely romantic about it.

I didn't wanna be caught in any kind of situation that would make me think of romance and Kyle in the same thought.

I forgot how handsome he was every time I saw him. The way the light played in his blue eyes, or when he smiled, and he showed off his teeth in a wide, predatory grin. I had to catch my breath and pretend his presence wasn't causing my heart to beat faster.

"Tell me, how have you been, Clarissa?" he asked after we were sitting at the table and our waitress took our drink order.

I looked at him and narrowed my eyes, trying to figure out what he was asking. Was there more to his question than simple, generic pleasantries? How much did I want to share with him? Did he deserve to get more than general small talk from me? How entangled into the details of my life did I want to take Kyle Love, and did he deserve to know that much about me?

"Life has had its ups and downs," I admitted. "How about you?"

He laughed. "Life has been a complete adventure. I am excited that it has taken me to some very interesting places. After all, I'm back in Chicago. Looks like James and I are going to come to an agreement, and I have the very good fortune of having dinner with you again."

He made it sound as if I were some kind of added bonus toy he was going to get by purchasing James's firm. If he was going to be around, maybe he needed to find out about all of the excessive details of my life. I still didn't plan on telling him about Leo, but there were other messes I could tell him about.

"Tell me why you're working for James."

I relaxed a little bit. Maybe this really was just an interview type situation where he wanted to find out about work life at the Stone Group. Maybe he wasn't interested in me on a personal level and didn't really care about how I had been the past few years since he left me. I took a sip of wine and steadied myself. I had to pause and think about it.

"Initially, I applied because it was a job in an architectural firm. Even though my school to job trajectory had changed rather dramatically for personal reasons, I still wanted to be in the world of architects" I admitted. "I no longer wanted to take on meaningless jobs so I could pay the rent. Even if I couldn't be an architect right away, it didn't mean I couldn't work for one when the opportunity presented itself. So, I went for it."

I continued to describe my process, how I ended up applying to several different architecture firms without ever letting Kyle know that I had spent several hard years out of work and ended up as a waitress and doing what I could to scrape by to support myself and my child.

"I got lucky and landed what I thought was a decent job right away. But their actual exceptions were not as they originally told me. There was some conflict, so I kept looking and ended up at the Stone Group. I've stayed with James because he proved to be a good boss. It's a small firm, and he treats us all like humans. If somebody has to take a day off, there's no question. They're allowed to. There's no drama about not being at your desk at a certain time or clocking in or staying until exactly five o'clock. He really understands that it's the people who work for him that make his business a success. He is a leader we all are willing to follow. He's not some kind of drill sergeant or task master who expects us to obey his command."

Kyle smiled and nodded and listened as I spoke.

The more I talked about working for James, the more I relaxed in Kyle's presence. I realized it was okay to not want a relationship with him anymore, and I didn't have to second-guess his motives. It was a nice moment of realizing I had grown up, and despite our past, I could be a civil person around Kyle. I didn't need to escape to another city to get away from him.

I almost completely forgot why Kyle had made me nervous before.

After he was done quizzing me about working with James, the conversation turned personal, but on a very surface level. I didn't feel the need to get emotional or philosophical with my answers.

"How did your studies go? Did you end up graduating?" he asked.

I took an unusually large gulp of wine and cleared my throat. "I graduated eventually." I sputtered and wiped my mouth with my napkin.

He lifted one eyebrow in question, a move I have always been envious of. "Eventually?"

"I returned to school in fall, expecting to be able to graduate the following spring. But I never finished my last semester. Some stuff happened, and I had to take a break for a year or two. I graduated from the program, and I have been taking classes to get my master's degree. I'm actually working the last course in my master's program this semester."

"And then what?" he asked.

I shrugged. There were too many possibilities for me to be able to give him a clear answer. However, one possibility I had been counting on, I no longer knew whether it was going to be possible or not.

"And then, hopefully, I will finally be an architect."

We were finished eating, and I didn't think Kyle needed to know any more about me.

"Thank you for dinner. It was good to see you. I hope I was able to answer your questions about working for James. You might want to offer to meet with his architect, Phillip, and draftsperson, Michelle. After all, I'm just a receptionist. I don't really work with him as much."

Kyle walked me out to the front of the restaurant.

"Can I walk you home?" he asked.

I shook my head. "No, I'll be fine. I live close by."

"Clarissa, are you sure? Let me call you a car," he said.

"I'm fine. I'm really only just a block away." I inwardly flinched when I said that. I didn't want him following me. He didn't need to know where I lived.

"I'm home," I announced when I walked in the door of my small apartment.

Marci unfolded herself from the couch and stood up. "How was dinner?"

I could tell from her expression that she was eager to know all the details. After all, she already knew everything.

"He wanted to know what it was like to work with James. There was no flirting, nothing that makes me think he's even interested."

"Are you okay?" she asked.

"I'm good," I said. "I'm actually glad. I don't want him to be interested."

"Why not? You know I'm happy to babysit when I can. And if you want to go on a date—"

"It wasn't a date," I said.

"If you say so. Like I was saying, if you want to go on a date with him, I will be here for you."

"Thank you for helping me out tonight. Now go home." I practically pushed her out my door.

She waved her fingers at me as she danced down the hall and into the apartment she shared with her boyfriend. Marci had been a great roommate, and I loved that we were still able to be neighbors.

Something Kyle had said over dinner stuck with me, and when I was back in the office on Monday morning, I went and saw James.

"Clarissa, what can I do for you?"

I stepped into my boss's office and sat down, twisting my fingers together nervously.

"I had a very interesting dinner with Kyle Love," I admitted. "He wanted to know what it was like to work for you."

I wasn't planning on keeping secrets from James, just as I wasn't planning on keeping secrets from Kyle as long as it was related to work.

"It sounds like you guys are coming to a rather quick deal," I said nervously. "He didn't tell me anything that I couldn't have asked you about, so I didn't think that would be an issue. But remember how you agreed to start my internship this semester?" I continued to twist my fingers together.

"Yes, I remember."

"Well, if you're selling the firm to Kyle, do you think he'll honor our agreement to allow me to work part-time and do the internship part-time?"

"You'd have to ask him that yourself," James said.

I bit my lip. I didn't want to ask Kyle for anything, but this was important.

"Clarissa, if he isn't willing to complete your internship or doesn't want to take you on as one, I'll help you find a situation with one of my colleagues. I won't leave you on your own for this. We had an agreement, and I'm the one changing everything, so it's the least I can do. Besides, I'm proud of you. You've really stuck with it."

16

KYLE

I was sitting at my desk reviewing a proposal on my laptop. I could hear Alayna in the outer office laughing with somebody. It was a little distracting, and I was having problems focusing on the proposal. I needed to power through this and get it back to the prospective client by the end of the week. If we were invited to the next round, this could be a very lucrative project for us.

I thought about getting up to close my office door but decided to double down on my concentration. I stayed in my chair and forced myself to read the words on my laptop. I wanted to at least get through this before I stopped for lunch. The talking in the outer office quieted, and I thought I was finally going to get some good quality work done when there was a knock on my office door.

It took me a moment to realize it wasn't Alayna standing there. I had to blink a couple of times before my brain caught up with my eyes. Standing there biting her lip looking as beautiful as she ever had been was Clarissa. Her hair was down around her shoulders, and her clothes were less severe than they had been the past couple of times I had seen her. She looked like the young woman who had grabbed my attention so long ago.

"What are you doing here?" I asked.

"I was wondering if you would be interested in letting me buy you lunch?" she asked.

I was always interested in lunch. And lunch with Clarissa seemed like a very intriguing prospect. "Lunch sounds like a good idea," I said.

"I wanted to talk to you about something," she admitted. "Is this an okay time?"

I shifted my gaze from her to the proposal on my laptop. I hit *Save* and closed the computer. "Now is a perfect time. I can't focus, so lunch sounds great," I said as I got to my feet.

"I'm buying, so don't expect anything fancy," she said as she walked out of the office. "It was really good to see you again," she said, pausing in front of Alayna's desk.

"You, too." Alayna gave her a smile.

As Clarissa stepped out of the office, Alayna turned to me with a 'what the hell is going on?' kind of expression. I shrugged and shook my head. I certainly didn't know what was going on.

We didn't say much as we walked down the street.

Clarissa stopped in front of a gyro shop. "I hope this is okay," she said as she opened the door for me.

"This is great. I haven't had Greek food in ages."

"I don't know if I would necessarily call this particularly authentic, but it sure is tasty," she said.

"Trust me, compared to what I got in Hong Kong, this is Greek," I said.

"Did they have Greek food in Hong Kong?" she asked.

"They have everything in Hong Kong. It's just not what I'm used to," I admitted. "For instance, I could get pizza, but it wasn't Chicago dish pizza."

"I don't think you can get that anywhere outside of Chicago," Clarissa agreed.

"Don't get me wrong, there is great food in Hong Kong. There's nothing like Hong Kong street food."

We waited in line before carrying orange plastic lunch trays with our sandwiches and drinks over to a small table with a beat-up Formica top and old wooden chairs. I bit into my sandwich and got lost in the play of flavors over my tongue. It was amazing. It was a whole sensory experience, not just the flavor and the texture. Food could bring back memories and feelings. There was nothing quite like savory lamb and beef with cucumber sauce mixed with tangy red onion and tomatoes. After several bites, I opened my eyes and looked up at Clarissa.

She was smiling at me. "You're really enjoying that, aren't you?" she asked.

I nodded and took a drink of my pop. "I haven't had one of these for years."

We both continued to eat our lunch without any chit chat before Clarissa started talking.

"I need to ask you a question. Well, it's not exactly a question." she paused. "I've got a possible problem."

I looked at her. She was so nervous that I was concerned that if I said something I would break her seemingly fragile ability to talk. She set her sandwich down and wiped her hands on a napkin.

"Did I tell you I'm finishing my studies this semester? I already made arrangements with James to do my final internship with the Stone Group, but..." She paused. She bit her upper lip the way she did when she was thinking. "Are you going to buy the Stone Group?" she blurted out.

"I'm thinking about it. It seems like it would be a good fit and a great way to instantly get reestablished in Chicago," I admitted.

She nodded and took a deep breath. Her chest strained the fabric at the front of her blouse. "You see, I have made arrangements with James to do my internship with the Stone Group, but if you take over… I asked him what he thought about being able to complete my internship with you. He said I needed to talk to you about it."

"About your becoming my intern?"

She nodded.

"What are your expectations here?" I asked. "How long is a semester?"

"Our semesters are fifteen weeks long, and for the program, they expect me to be in an internship for ten to twelve weeks full-time."

"The last time I accepted interns, there was paperwork involved," I said.

"Yeah, but the application for the Stone Group has already been submitted and approved. I guess it depends on whether you take over completely before the end of next semester. There is an assessment you would need to fill out and turn in."

"And after the internship, then what?"

She grimaced. "I leave the Stone Group and go find a job. It's been drilled into us not to expect anything to come from the internship. Besides, it's not like James would hire me for a junior position. He doesn't have any openings, and now he's selling it all off to retire."

"Let me see if I understand this. You're going to quit being the receptionist to become an intern?" I asked.

She shook her head. "Not exactly. The thing is, because I have to work," she continued, "and since I already work for the architectural firm where I will be doing my internship, the program coordinator at the university has allowed me to do my internship with part-time hours but for a longer time— more than a single semester, so I still get the same amount of hours for the credits."

"And James is okay with that?"

"He was reluctant at first," she admitted. "But when he realized that I was going to eventually leave, he agreed to it. This way, I'm still around a little longer. I can't be a receptionist for the rest of my life. I've spent too many years working toward this degree." She was flush with excitement. Suddenly, she seemed to become shy, and she looked down at her hands. "It's taking a long time, and my career trajectory didn't go the way I planned, but I'm still just as eager and excited to become an architect as I was before…" She trailed off. She broke off a piece of her sandwich and put it in her mouth.

It seemed like she was leaving something out.

"When is this internship supposed to start? At the beginning of next semester?" I asked.

Clarissa took a sip of her drink and shook her head. "Because of my special circumstances, the internship starts just after midterms."

"And when is that?"

She bit her lip and crinkled up her nose. "In two weeks."

No wonder she was nervous.

"What's the plan?" I asked.

"I'll be the firm's receptionist part-time in the mornings, and then in the afternoons, I'll be James's intern. He's agreed to continue to pay me my full salary the entire time. If you aren't willing to work with me under the same arrangements… Well, because of our history…" she said.

I nodded in understanding.

"So, anyway, if you can't or won't, I understand. No hard feelings. But I need to know. James said he would help me find an internship with one of his colleagues and help me to find a paying one since I cannot afford to not work for a full semester at this point in my life. I have to be able to pay rent, you know?"

I waved my hand and shook my head in a stopping gesture. "You don't have to worry about any of that. You don't need to change your plans simply because the Stone Group is changing ownership. I've worked with you in the past. I'm willing to take you on as an intern again."

She let out a deep sigh of relief. "Oh, thank you. That's wonderful. Thank you," she said. "Are you finished?" She reached out for my plastic tray covered in empty sandwich wrappers.

I rattled my ice in the paper cup and took one last slurp of my pop before putting it on the tray. "All set," I said.

I waited for her at the door as she took care of our garbage.

"You know, I expected everything to be different when I return to Chicago, but it seems like everything is the same. Nothing's changed." I chuckled.

"What do you mean?" she asked.

"I'm back in Chicago after six years. The food is just as good as I remembered it, and you are still my intern."

17

CLARISSA

I wasn't privy to all the details when it came to the sale of the Stone Group to Kyle Love. I just knew that he started to be in our offices more and more at some point. The transition was so seamless that none of us really noticed. Or at least I think that's what the plan was. Everything seemed to take place around the same time my internship was scheduled to begin.

My first official day as Jame's intern started off not too much different from any normal workday. Except when I left for lunch, the front desk was taken over by a temp.

"Go be an intern, I've got this," Jenna said as she shooed me off toward James's office and began showing the new woman how we expected things to be handled.

Before I had a chance to even wonder what I was supposed to do for my first day as intern, Kyle swept into James's office and announced that he was taking the new intern for the rest of the day.

James sat back and gestured at me like I was some kind of commodity. "There she is."

"What's going on?" I was more than a little concerned.

"James has worked with you for several years. He knows what you think about architecture. He knows what to expect from you," Kyle said.

"So do you." At least he did six years ago. "You had me show you around some of my favorite architectural places in Chicago."

Kyle grinned at me. I was too annoyed to be swayed by his charming grin.

"Give me a reminder," he crooned. He was trying to be suave. I refused to fall for him.

"Are you going to let him kidnap me like this?" I asked James.

He chuckled, thinking I was being funny. "I'm certain it'll be a good start for getting you into the right mindset. Get out of the office. Clear your head."

I cast my gaze from James to Kyle and back again.

"Are you serious?"

"Get your coat. Come on," Kyle said with a tilt to his head.

I had no choice but to follow him out of the office. I bit my tongue until we were outside.

"What kind of game do you think you're playing?" I demanded to know.

"I want to see if your architectural taste has changed at all. Will you take me to the same places, show me the same details?"

I glared at him.

"Relax, Clarissa. I thought this would give us a chance to get reacquainted, give me a chance to see if your ideals have changed at all. I feel like there is more than a few years between us that I've somehow missed. I thought we could reconnect."

I stopped walking. Kyle took a few more steps before he realized I was no longer keeping up with him. I stared down at the sidewalk. There was so much more than a few lost years between us.

I sucked in a deep breath and raised my eyes. I stared at him. It was hard to read his expression with half of his face hidden behind aviator sunglasses. I took a long look at Kyle. Yes, he was incredibly handsome, and he broke my heart, but that didn't mean I had to let him get that close to me again.

The gap between us was a trench of his own making. And now he wanted to reconnect? There were so many things I could say right now.

"You never gave me a chance to thank you in person and say goodbye," I managed to say. It was the least dramatic of the things on my long list of complaints that were in that chasm between us.

"I got caught up in the project," he said. "I was harnessing the power of hyper focus. It's one of the things that helped me get to where I am."

"Your sense of design and personality got you where you are. Your hyper focus is just an excuse for when you stopped talking to me." I kept my voice low. I wasn't going to yell, but he needed to know he had hurt me. He had no idea what his disappearance had done to my ego and self-esteem, not a single clue about the struggle it had been to not give everything up. I don't know how I would've made it if it hadn't been for Marci, the best friend I could have ever dreamed of having.

He nodded slowly. "I could have handled that better."

Was that his idea of an apology? I didn't know if it was or not, but we couldn't stand here all day hashing out our past. He wanted me to show him something. Fine. I'd show him something.

"I'm not dressed for taking a walking tour. These shoes are not made for walking all over the city," I pointed out before I started to walk again.

He continued to stroll down the block, completely unfazed by my griping. He stopped and opened a door to a pizza place.

"Why are we here?" I paused before stepping inside.

"I haven't eaten. Have you?"

He certainly did like his food. We both seemed to momentarily forget about our grievances and agreed there was nothing quite like a good Chicago pizza. At least we could agree on something. The food had somehow helped me reach some form of inner truce. He knew I was upset. That was a start.

After lunch, Kyle called a cab, but instead of telling it to take us to the river and into the loop to see the buildings I had shown him that first little tour we had taken, I asked the driver to drop us off in Oak Park. The little secret temples were still my architectural happy places. They were the recognizable details that film makers went for when setting a movie in Chicago. If they didn't use the towering glass façade of the Willis Tower, they were using action shots around the Tribune Tower with its flying buttresses. But Kyle didn't need me to show those to him again.

He didn't say anything until after we both climbed out of the car and it left. "I'm surprised you chose to show me Frank Lloyd Wright houses," Kyle said.

"Who says we're here to look at Frank Lloyd Wright? There are other architectural works in the neighborhood."

"We're in Oak Park," Kyle said as if I needed a reminder.

It was a nice fall day. Kyle's jacket hung open, and he shoved his hands deep into his pockets. Leaves crunched underfoot.

"If we're not here to look at Frank Lloyd Wright"—he gestured at a house we approached— "Then why are we here? I thought you said you weren't up for walking."

"I'm not up for walking at the high-speed clip expected of me if we were downtown. I can handle a little stroll around the neighborhood."

Kyle slowed his pace and cocked his elbow out toward me. There was something about that gesture that felt more like an olive branch than any words he could have spoken.

I accepted the invitation and slid my hand into the crook of his arm.

"We're only about a block away from the house I want to show you." It sat next to a Frank Lloyd Wright house. It wasn't famous, but it was lovely.

"I've done the unofficial tours in Oak Park more times than I care to remember. I've seen this house so many times, and I came to realize how much I liked the fine details. It doesn't have a hidden temple on top, and it seems to be several decades older, or maybe the Frank Lloyd Wright house was just ahead of it. But you can see the transition from the late Victorian style transitions into Craftsman style. Architecturally, this house is underappreciated. Ask anyone about the houses on either side of the famous ones. No one is going to remember it."

We stood on the sidewalk and looked at the house. I didn't think the neighbors would have been too concerned. They were more than used to people walking through and gawking at the other homes.

"Why have you picked this one to show me?" Kyle asked.

"I think as the people who design buildings and public spaces, we need to not be so blinded by the flash and glam that we miss out on charm, functionality."

"I seem to recall you weren't a fan of form follows function."

"I'm not a fan of function limiting the style. I'm saying that it's the little things that make something endearing. Look, just because something is popular and famous, doesn't mean it's necessarily the better solution."

Kyle crossed his arms and turned toward me. "This isn't about houses or schools of style, is it?"

I snorted. "Sorry, but I'm not so deep as to have formulated some kind of architectural metaphor on our relationship from the time we ate lunch until now. If you are reading anything into what I have chosen to show you, maybe you need to reflect on why you think that way." I took a few steps away, leaving him to glare at me. "Come on, I love this area. Besides, if I'm going to show you Frank Lloyd Wright buildings, you know I have to show you his temple. You already know how I feel about those."

"You do love little temples, don't you?" he asked as he jogged a few steps to catch up.

18

KYLE

The transition of taking over Stone Group was a relatively painless process. The offices were a little crowded as my team slowly began to move in. With the invaluable help of James's office manager, Jenna, Alayna did her magic, and we were able to secure a lease for additional space on the floor above us.

Since we were already an architectural firm, we were able to handle our own expansion design. We only needed to bring in an outside firm to complete structural analysis for putting in a staircase.

It was a fabulous first project for Clarissa since she was involved from the very first planning discussions. The full team was gathered in the conference room as we reviewed sketches that everybody collectively worked on. Stone Group's team, Phillip the architect, and their draftsperson, Michelle, were discussing their wants and needs with my guys, Nick and Steve.

The addition of the space directly above us would allow our office space to more than double, and nobody would have to relocate offices if they didn't want to.

"We're gonna lose James's office," Clarissa said as she pointed to one set of sketches.

"It's not like James is going to be here all the time," Phillip added.

"I'll be here often enough that I still need an office," James replied.

"Move your office upstairs. Your square footage will double." I wasn't paying exact attention to who was saying what.

"But if we put the stairs down here in James's office, they'll come out right next to the restrooms upstairs. I'm not sure if we really want stairs leading directly to the restrooms."

"Our other option is to lose the conference room, which is in the farthest corner of our space right now."

Steve reached over and lined the two sets of plans up next to each other. "Our choices are that we have an aesthetically pleasing staircase on the main floor, or we have an aesthetically pleasing staircase location on the second. We can't do both. We're limited by the space we have and the building we're in."

"How much will clients need to see? We need a conference room for them to meet in, right?" Clarissa asked.

"Yeah, and we need one to spread out and do work like this," Nick said.

"We can put a conference room upstairs," Michelle suggested.

"Do we really want to make our clients have to walk upstairs to get to a conference room?"

I leaned back and let the team hash it out. I had my opinions on the whole thing, and I knew James had his opinions. Neither of us said anything. It was important to see how our newly combined team worked together to problem solve. Steve and Phillip stood next to each other. It was almost as if I could see their processes in tandem.

"We could turn the entire upstairs into an open office work plan," Steve started.

"Oh, hell no. I want walls. I need to be able to close a door," Michelle snapped. "Do not put me in one of those open office concepts."

Phillip tapped his finger on the plans. "Okay, so instead of a complete open office concept, we go with some kind of modification. Something that gives us privacy if needed, and also, collaborative working space."

"We could put in movable walls."

"Only if they are real walls and not some kind of folding thick curtains like they use in conference centers. Those are ugly and barely provide privacy. I'd almost rather have a garage door."

"So, are we discussing moving all the creatives upstairs and leaving down here for administrative offices and the conference room?" Phillip asked.

Steve started nodding. "Yeah, we leave the administrative offices downstairs and turn upstairs into an architectural playground."

"Where does my office go?" I asked.

Phillip made a circle with his finger over the area that was James's current office. "If we put the stairs here and Michelle and I move upstairs, we can then knock down this wall and open all of this up. That becomes your office."

"When a client comes to visit," Clarissa started, "they would see your big, impressive office, a beautiful staircase leading upstairs, and this conference room. And only if they were interested in seeing where the actual work gets done would they go upstairs. At that point, it's on them if they get upset that the first door they see is a restroom."

"I don't have a problem with it as long as I have a door that I can close," Michelle announced.

Michelle and Nick left the meeting first. They both had deadlines they needed to focus on. Steve and Phillip began shuffling the drawings into some semblance of order.

"You had some very good questions today, Clarissa," James said. "You need to keep thinking outside the box, especially when everybody else"—he pointed at her and then he circled his finger around, indicating everybody else in the room— "is caught up in the details that they want. Keep asking questions to bring it all back to the bigger picture. What are the usage needs going forward? Don't be afraid to ask clients these things." He patted her on the shoulder and smiled as he walked out.

"Good job," I said.

She turned her smile to me, and I felt an odd sensation deep in my chest that I hadn't experienced in a very long time. As I was about to open my mouth and ask her out to dinner, she looked down at her phone and gasped.

"I'm late. I have to go. I will see everyone tomorrow," she said, running out the door.

Philip didn't seem to notice anything, but Steve let out a low laugh.

"What are you laughing about?" I asked.

"Oh, nothing," he said.

"I call bullshit. Why are you laughing at Clarissa?" I pushed.

"I was just thinking she's still cute. You know I had a little bit of a crush on her back when we interned for you before."

I must have flinched or looked at him with a shocked expression.

"You don't have to worry about anything. I don't think she even noticed. And she certainly wouldn't notice now."

I pointed at him. "Don't develop a crush on my intern."

Phillip looked up from rolling drawings and scoffed. "Don't look at me," he said. "I won't report this conversation to HR. You might not want to say anything the next time Michelle is around. She gets very peculiar about appropriate office behavior."

"Noted," I said while giving Steve a knowing glance.

I made a mental note for myself as well. *Do not be inappropriate with the intern.* It was a hard lesson that I really hadn't learned the last time Clarissa had been my intern.

"Good morning," I muttered as I pushed my way into the office the next day.

Clarissa was already behind the receptionist desk. "Good morning. Alayna is already here. She has some information for you. James left a message. He said he'll meet you at your client meeting. He's not gonna come in today. If you need to spread out in his office for any reason, feel free to do that."

"Thanks," I said. "You took off pretty quickly last night."

"I was late for a meeting," she said.

There was something off about the tone of her voice and I didn't quite think she was telling me the truth, but I also knew it wasn't my place to ask.

"What are you doing for dinner tonight?" I asked, completely ignoring my own advice of the evening before of not getting involved with the intern.

"It's Friday. I'm making spaghetti."

"Do you make spaghetti every Friday?" I asked.

She bit her lip and looked to the side, thinking. "I guess I do. I don't have to think about it. I just know that I make spaghetti."

"What do you have for dinner on Mondays?"

"Usually, chicken," she said.

"Do you cook every night?"

"I don't cook every night. Sometimes, we have pizza," she admitted.

"We?" I asked.

"I have a roommate," she blurted out.

"Not the same one you had before?" I asked.

Clarissa giggled. "No, I don't live with Marci anymore, even though we're still in the same building."

"You're still friends?"

"Best friends," she said with a smile.

"That must be convenient," I said.

The phone rang.

"I've gotta get this," she said as she reached for the receiver.

I left her to her work.

Clarissa was still sitting behind the desk and waved as I left for my meeting with James and his client right before lunch. The meeting went as well. The client seemed genuinely pleased that James would still be involved with the business for at least the next year. I was confident that I had made the right choice of buying out the Stone Group.

When I returned to the office, Clarissa was still at the receptionist desk.

"Why are you sitting there?" I asked.

Clarissa let out an aggravated sound. "The receptionist didn't come in. She didn't even call, and she hasn't returned any of my calls. I don't know whether I should be angry or worried."

"You've been doing your old job all day?"

"Exactly, and not that measuring the empty offices upstairs is a whole lot of fun, but it's what I was supposed to be doing today. Instead, I've just been sitting here waiting for the phone to ring."

"Why don't you set the phones to voicemail and come and have a drink with me?"

"I have to be somewhere by six," she said.

"The same meeting you had yesterday?"

She nodded.

"It's only four thirty. You have plenty of time," I pointed out.

"But the office doesn't close for another hour."

"I'm the boss. Close early. Come on, Clarissa, one little drink."

"Fine, one drink, but nothing alcoholic," she insisted.

"We can go to the coffee shop if you want." I gave her my best pleading expression. How could she resist me?

"I shouldn't, but okay," she gave in.

"Great, be ready to go in fifteen minutes."

19

CLARISSA

I can't believe I agreed to go out for coffee with Kyle. Nerves in my stomach rioted in an entirely too familiar way. It would be so easy to slip back into our old habits. He was funny and charming, and I spent entirely too much time giggling.

"You really did well in the meeting today," he said.

It had felt good when James had said that, but when Kyle said it… somehow, it meant more. I tried and failed at not blushing. I knew this couldn't be anything more than colleagues wrapping up the end of a long work week. I reminded myself that this was all this was allowed to be. But I was too wound up, too nervous. Relief flooded my body when the alarm on my phone went off.

"I've got to go," I announced as I scrambled to pull my things together.

"Are you sure?" He placed his hand over the top of mine. "Stay a little bit longer."

"I really can't. I had a nice time," I admitted.

"Have dinner with me this weekend," he demanded.

I cast my gaze to the side. I bit my lip and looked anywhere but at him. "Maybe."

I should've said no. But part of me wanted to have a nice adult conversation that didn't involve work, and part of me just wanted to see Kyle again. "I'll see if I can figure something out," I said. "I'll text you tomorrow?"

As much as I was going to be late picking up Leo, it felt like I was running away from Kyle. I didn't wanna run away from Kyle, and that was problematic.

I knew it was.

"How's my big boy?" I asked as soon as I walked into the daycare.

"Mommy!" Leo already had his jacket on, and his bag was packed and waiting by the door. I knew it was because I was almost too late.

Miss Franny looked at her wall clock and then at me. "You just barely made it."

"I know. I'm so sorry. I got stuck at work." A drink with my boss counted as work, right?

I helped Leo with his backpack and held his hand as he walked next to me.

"We're having spaghetti for dinner," I told him as we walked home.

"Spaghetti is my favorite food!" Leo exclaimed.

I was glad to hear he still liked it. That was one of the reasons we had it practically every Friday. He would eat it.

If I had said we were having chicken nuggets, he would've said chicken nuggets were his favorite food. With Leo, something was either his favorite or he hated it and it was gross. He didn't seem to be a fussy eater, but I still tried to work within his preferences. It was one less thing I had to stress about. And I wasn't exactly heartbroken to not have to fight him over eating broccoli when he was just as happy to eat a bowl full of salad.

Once home, we settled in for our Friday night routine. I made spaghetti. I wasn't a fancy cook, and I used sauce out of a jar. It was good, filling, and cheap. After dinner, Leo played in the tub, and I got almost as wet as he did. He put his pajamas on, and then we cuddled up on the couch to watch a movie.

Friday night movies meant we were going to watch mutant turtles, talking shape shifting robots, or dinosaurs breaking out of their enclosures. We rarely watched anything else. They were Leo's comfort movies after a week at school. Tonight, he wanted robots.

He curled up against me, and while the robots on TV turned into airplanes and plotted to save the planet, I was on my phone texting Marci.

Can you babysit???? I needed all of the question marks. This was a very important question.

What's up?

Dinner with Kyle.

She responded with a series of emojis that ranged from exploding heads to smiley faces with hearts for eyes, followed by several eggplants and several peaches. I didn't know if I could take her less than subtle innuendo. I didn't even know if this was a date. I didn't plan on sleeping with the man.

I doubt it, I replied.

She wrote back, *I have condoms. I'll bring them over. What time?*

I guess that meant I was available for dinner with Kyle.

Completely oblivious to the turmoil I was going through, Leo fell asleep about halfway through the movie. I was a bad mother because it was at least thirty minutes before I realized that he was asleep. I was so preoccupied with texting Marci and setting up a time to meet Kyle that I hadn't even noticed. Leo was comfortable and I wasn't bothering him, so I let him sleep as I continued to plan for my dinner out.

Where is he taking you? Marci asked.

I don't know'

You need to so you know how to dress. She had a point.

I'll just dress normally, I responded.

No, you will not!!!!!!! The extra exclamation points only emphasized her intensity.

You're going on a date with the father of your son, who you haven't seen in years.

I don't know if it's a date.

It's a date! she responded.

As I was reading Marci's message, another text message popped up. *I'm glad to hear you're available. Should I pick you up or do you wanna meet at the restaurant?*

My stomach flipped when I saw Kyle's message.

I thought I was still responding to Marci when I typed and sent, *I don't think it's a date.*

Only to have Kyle respond with, *I don't plan on talking business with you. Yes, it's a date.*

I dropped my phone on my lap and covered my eyes, wanting to die of embarrassment. After a long moment to regain my composure, I very carefully typed out to Kyle. *Thank you for clarifying. This is a date. I will meet you at the restaurant. Will seven thirty be good?*

Then I switched to the message thread with Marci. *OMG, he just said yes it's a date. I sent a message meant for you to him.*

Dying, yay.

The next afternoon, Marci sat on my bed with Leo while I paraded around in another outfit.

I put together a basic black, understated outfit. I was trying to look somewhat classy and not like somebody who was tired and worn out.

"You can't wear that," Marci said.

"Why not? It's a classic, basic black."

"Oh, sweetie, black makes you look washed out and really brings out the bags under your eyes. It makes you look tired."

"I am tired," I confessed.

"You should take a nap," Leo said from where he played in the middle of the bed among all the discarded clothes I had already pulled out of my closet. He was right, I needed a nap. But I had needed a nap for the past six years. I didn't have any time to catch up on sleep now.

Marci started going through the pile on my bed. She held up a blouse I hadn't even bothered to try on. "How about this yellow blouse and a pair of jeans?"

"I can't wear that on a date," I said.

"What's the date?" Leo asked.

My insides clenched. I didn't want him to know about Kyle. And it wasn't as if I had gone on any dates since the last time I had been with him.

"A date is a number on a calendar," Marci said.

Leo seemed to accept that as an answer.

"Kids are so easy at this age." She giggled.

"The yellow is nice, but isn't that too summery?"

"Just because it's fall doesn't mean you can't wear something bright and like sunshine." She held it up against my chest. "You look rested with this color."

She pulled the blouse away, leaving me in the black one. She did this a few times. "You can keep the skirt, just go put this one on."

I finished getting dressed in the bathroom.

"Don't forget to curl your hair!" she called out through the bathroom door.

I took the time to flat iron and curl my hair, something I hadn't done for years. By the time I stepped out of the bathroom, I felt like I looked pretty.

"What do you think?" I twirled back and forth in the middle of the living room.

"Mommy, you look like a girl," Leo said. The way he said it made me think that maybe he didn't think girls were a good thing.

"I am a girl," I said. "So I guess it's a good thing I look like one."

Marci scrambled off the couch and grabbed her purse. "Wait, I have something for you."

She pulled a blue box from her purse and slid it into my bag.

I closed my eyes and tried not to blush as she slipped me the condoms.

"Have fun, stay out late!" She pushed me out the door.

I was so nervous, I thought I might be sick. But all of my nerves evaporated when I arrived at the restaurant. Kyle was waiting for me, and when he saw me, his entire expression changed. I forgot everything I had been stressing over and felt a sense of belonging.

"You look beautiful," he said, stepping up and giving me a kiss on the cheek.

I placed my hand over the spot, holding it for a moment.

We followed the hostess to our table. Unlike the brightly lit, family friendly Italian place we had dinner at a few weeks earlier, this place was dimly lit, with tables tucked into dark, secluded alcoves. This place was dangerous. After a glass of wine, I was feeling dangerous as well.

20

KYLE

I sat there watching Clarissa slide the spoon full of creamy dessert into her mouth. The way her lips wiped away the crème brûlée made it difficult to swallow. I leaned forward.

"If you're attempting to tease me, you should know that it's working. I wouldn't mind if you agreed to enjoy me as thoroughly."

She pressed her lips together and a blush tinted her cheeks.

I sat back and took the last sip of wine in my glass. "Will you let me walk you home this evening?"

She shook her head even though a smile played across her lips.

"Are you willing to come home with me?"

"I was hoping you'd ask," she said.

I couldn't get out of the restaurant fast enough. I practically threw my credit card at the waitress as I dragged Clarissa out of there. I barely let her finish her dessert.

It may not have been as dramatic as described, but I no longer had the patience for a long game.

Once we were in the back of a cab, I leaned in for a kiss.

She pushed me away, casting nervous glances at the back of the driver's head. "Not here."

I let myself be temporarily satisfied with holding her wrist and placing kisses on her fingers and her palm.

"You live in the same place?" she asked as she climbed out of the car once we arrived.

"Why do you sound surprised?" I pulled her back against my chest and began nuzzling against her ear.

"You've been out of the country."

"I leased it out. Come inside," I choked out, almost unable to speak with my need to get her inside.

I didn't pause and took her straight to the bedroom. I pulled her tight into my arms for the first time in more years than I cared to remember. I properly kissed her. Her lips like the sweetest ambrosia that I had been missing. Her body pressed against mine felt like the home I didn't realize I had completely forgotten but now needed to reclaim. The details of how I got her out of her clothes or how I managed to get out of mine were lost. I was frantic, unable to catch my breath until I held her soft skin against mine.

As I prepared to lower her to the bed, she flinched. "Are you okay?"

"Just a moment," she said as she scrambled to her feet and across the room to where she had dropped her purse. She returned holding out a box of condoms.

I took the box from her and looked at her.

"I came prepared. You need to use one," she told me.

"I never did before."

"Well, things have changed," she told me.

I took and ripped the box open. I pulled out a couple of packets and threw them on the pillow.

"Where were we?" I murmured as my lips found the soft skin of her neck.

She practically purred under my lips.

No other woman ever felt the way Clarissa did in my arms. I had been a fool to walk away from her. That was not a mistake I planned on letting happen again.

She whimpered the sexiest sounds that went straight to my balls, making them tight and ready for release. She tasted better than any dessert or wine I could have had.

She clutched me to her as my lips trailed over her skin. There weren't words that could properly describe her breasts or the way they were tipped with dark pink nipples. Her skin was sweeter than any berry or spun sugar.

I devoured her, sucking one nipple into my mouth to tease with my tongue before repeating the attention to her other nipple. My hands roamed across her soft skin. I needed to touch every part of her. I grabbed onto her soft hips and kneaded and massaged as I tried to palm her very essence into my hands. My hands stroked down her ribs, and I cupped her bountiful breasts while I sank into her.

My lips would wander, and I kissed across her abdomen before shifting to place a kiss on one delightful knee. I kept returning to her hot mouth, claiming her. She sucked my tongue into her mouth, and I gave her everything just as she was giving herself to me.

My cock slid over her folds. She gasped as my head bumped against the cluster of nerves in her clit.

"You like?" I growled.

She whimpered and shook her head, letting out more moans of pleasure as I directed my erection over and around her eager pussy. I pressed the tip into her, and she bucked.

"Condom!"

"I will, but let me have just a taste first." I eased into her slowly. I didn't make it halfway in before I realized that was a wonderful feeling but a very bad idea. I pulled back and found one of the accursed things. I ripped the packet open and slid the condom on.

I fell back to her body, ready to reclaim her. Even as it felt as if I were consuming her, she wrapped around me and pulled me into her wet, hot body.

My cock slid into her pussy with such precision, as if it had been long anticipated and more than welcome. Our bodies fit together as if we had been made for each other.

Clarissa writhed and pulsed and cried out.

I pushed up on my arms so I could look down at her. Her eyes were closed, and her lips parted as she panted beneath me. I thrust deep into her, wanting all of me to be taken into her. Yet, I needed my mouth on her. I lowered to her breast and pulled a peaked nipple into my mouth. I sucked and teased her with my tongue with the same timing that I thrust and pushed against her core.

This was all give, all take. I surrendered my body completely to hers, and she gave herself to me. Her body tensed. She counter thrust hard, and she clenched up. It was almost as if her body wanted to fight against mine.

She threw her head back and gasped. "Kyle, Kyle, I… harder… I need more!"

Her wish was my command. I drove into her with an urgent need. It was as if I was trying to get somewhere deep inside her, someplace magical and perfect.

She clenched down on my cock with a force I hadn't felt before. Her orgasm was like a wild ride as she bucked, and her body sucked at mine. And then I exploded. I was there. I had achieved perfection with her. I could barely breathe as lights exploded around us. My cock pumped into her, and it felt like that action was the very purpose of my existence.

It wasn't quite midnight when I rolled over and noticed the bed was empty. I sat up. "Clarissa?"

She stepped out of the bathroom, adjusting her clothes, as I called her name.

"Are you leaving?"

"I can't stay. As much as I'd like to, I can't."

Disappointment pierced me in the chest. "Is there something I can do to change your mind?"

She stepped over and leaned into me. I wanted to wrap my arms around her and pull her back into bed.

"I wish there was, but no, I've got to go." She pressed her lips to mine in the sweetest goodbye. "I'll see you on Monday," she said before she left.

I couldn't get back to sleep, wondering what was going on in her life that she needed to leave me. I had just gotten her back.

I spent the next day wondering what was going on in Clarissa's life that she couldn't stay the night. I couldn't focus on anything. Unable to think of anything better to do, I took myself on a long walk. I found myself standing in front of London House, looking up at the cupola.

I ended up going to all of the buildings, including the little Victorian tucked between high-rise apartments, that Clarissa had shown me.

I got on the train and found myself walking through Oak Park. It was a nice neighborhood. The old houses were perfect for families. I didn't remember the house that Clarissa had shown me, but I spent time actually looking at the little details I thought she would appreciate or might point out to me.

The screaming laughter of small children caught my attention as I strolled past a neighborhood park. I stopped and had to shake my head to clear my vision when I thought I saw the familiar form of Clarissa holding hands with a small child.

That couldn't be her. Could it? Who was that kid she was with?

He ran over to her, holding out a large orange leaf. She took it and leaned in. Her lips pursed for a kiss. The little boy grimaced and pushed at her. He took a few running steps away as he escaped her, only to turn and run right back to her, throwing his arms around her and pressing his face into her. She kissed the top of his head, and he ran off again.

I immediately turned in the opposite direction, not wanting her to see me. I had to figure all of this out. Was that kid the reason she couldn't stay? I growled as anger boiled in my gut. That kid and his father, most likely. I was a fool. It was bad enough that I seduced the intern again. This time, it looked like I hadn't bothered to learn whether she was single or not.

21

CLARISSA

"Good morning," I practically sang the second Kyle walked through the doors.

I had been dancing on clouds all weekend ever since I left him, and his smile first thing Monday morning was going to guarantee I had a good week. Or so I thought. He glanced up and noticed I was there. But he didn't look at me and he didn't say anything. He didn't smile, didn't wink. He didn't stop and say anything that could have been laced with innuendo.

He simply walked past me and into the back.

Everything inside me wanted to run after him at that moment. So of course, with perfect annoying timing, the phone rang. I stayed at my desk and took messages instead of finding out whether I had done something wrong.

As he and James left for lunch together, James did his typical finger tap on my desk followed by a wave, letting me know he was leaving without interrupting his conversation. Kyle didn't even glance up at me. I scowled at his back as they left.

"Yikes, don't tell me that look is for me."

I cut a glare to Nick as he approached the receptionist desk. "What are you talking about?" I snapped.

Nick drew a circle in the air with his finger in front of his face. "That look," he said, meaning my expression.

I tried to regain my composure. "Oh, sorry," I said. "Why would I be scowling at you? Why do you think that was for you?"

"I figured they just told you that you were stuck with me all afternoon."

"That actually could prove to be interesting as long as the afternoon temp remembers to come in," I grumbled.

"Oh, yeah, I heard about that. What happened?"

I shrugged. "The agency called this morning. They're sending somebody new."

Nick did a similar tapping on the desk thing. "Well, I'm off to lunch. Come find me when you're good to go."

"Where will you be?" I asked.

"If I'm not in my office, I'll be upstairs."

My intern duties were relegated to Nick's supervision for the rest of the week. Which was just as well because I was pretty certain Kyle was angry and was avoiding me.

I didn't have a chance to talk to him for a couple of days. "Did I do something to piss you off?" I asked him the second he walked in the door a few mornings later. I wasn't going to give him a chance to continue ignoring me.

He stopped and leveled a glare at me. "Do you have something you need to tell me?"

Confused, I shook my head. "No, I... What? No. What is going on, Kyle?"

He stalked menacingly toward my desk and leaned over it, getting close to my face. He was trying to be intimidating. It was working. "Are you sure you don't want to tell me something?"

"Was I supposed to send you an engraved thank you note after Saturday night?" I snapped back.

He shook his head, letting out a bitter chuckle. "No, but maybe you should have told me you're in a relationship."

Now I was really confused. "I don't know what you're talking about."

He was still leaning over my desk when Alayna stepped in. "This looks like a situation that needs to not be happening right here in the reception area."

Kyle turned his glare at her, which shocked me because I was pretty certain he thought Alayna could do no wrong. It was nice to know that she had the confidence. It must have been nice to have the confidence and authority to put him in check.

He cleared his throat a couple of times and then stood up straight. "You're right." He looked back at me. "This is not a conversation I care to have right now."

I folded my arms over my chest. "Fine, but this is a conversation that needs to happen."

Alayna looked like a stern schoolteacher. She wagged her finger at us as if we were naughty children. "Whatever is going on right here, you two need to figure it out and get it cleared up before anybody starts asking me what's going on."

I didn't know if she knew what was going on between us or that we even had a history. I nodded. She was right. We needed to get this cleared up.

Kyle grunted and stormed off into the back office.

As I watched Alayna walk away, I realized there was no way she didn't not know there was something going on. She seemed to know everything.

For some reason, I hoped Kyle would have approached me to meet outside the office to discuss whatever he was so upset about. By the end of the work week, I was left with more questions than I had answers for.

Leo and I followed our standard Friday evening routine. I picked him up from daycare. I made spaghetti for dinner, and after a bath, we watched a movie. My phone pinged with a text. It was Marci.

What, no date this weekend??? Three question marks.

No, was all I responded.

I expected her to text me back. Less than five minutes later, she was knocking on my door and yelling at me to let her in.

"What's going on?" she asked as soon as I got the door open.

"Nothing's going on," I said with a shrug.

"You should be getting ready for a date. Why didn't you ask me to babysit? I even told Davey we couldn't go out tomorrow night because I was expecting to babysit."

I grimaced. "I guess you can tell Davey he can take you out."

"Well, what happened? I thought you were going to talk to him?"

I had let Marci know that Kyle had a stick up his ass over something. "I tried to, but we got scolded by his personal assistant because we were not being professional."

Marci and I spoke in aggressive whispers so as to not disrupt Leo and his movie. Fortunately, the dinosaurs on the TV were louder than we were. Marci opened my refrigerator and pulled out a bottle of wine. I grabbed the cups from the cupboard as she unscrewed the top off a cheap wine and poured.

She took a sip and waggled her eyebrows at me. That was my cue to tell her what was going on. I needed to talk.

"I asked him if he was pissed off at me, and he is," I told her.

"But why?"

"I don't know. He seems to think I'm dating somebody else. "

"Did he see you with somebody? Anybody?"

I shrugged. "Between Saturday night and Sunday, the only person I've been with is my son. He wasn't acting like he saw me with some kid. He was acting like he saw me with another man."

"Do you have a doppelganger we don't know about? Did you go to the grocery store? Did you say thank you to a delivery man?"

I had no answers.

"Give me your phone."

"What? No," I said as she grabbed it off the kitchen counter.

With deft ninja-like skills, Marci grabbed my wrist and had my thumbprint unlocking my phone before I could snatch my hand away from her.

I watched with a combination of resolve and horror as I knew she was texting Kyle.

"There." She held the phone out to me.

I read the message that I supposedly sent. *What's going on? We need to talk on Saturday.* She had the name of a bar and a time listed.

"You are going to go and wait for him, and I'm going to babysit," she announced right before she gulped down the rest of her wine, said goodnight to Leo, and left.

She was a force of nature. I was glad she was on my side.

The next evening, I sat on a bar stool. The ice in my drink was melting as I waited for Kyle.

"I'm here," he announced as he slid onto the bar stool next to me.

"I didn't think you were coming," I said. In an attempt to look like a badass, I took a sip of my drink. The effect was completely ruined as I grimaced and shuddered at the bitter vodka in my Moscow Mule.

Kyle gestured for the bartender. "I'll have one of those," he said, pointing at my drink.

"What the hell is going on?" I asked.

"Are you seeing anybody?"

"I thought I was seeing you," I responded.

"That's not what I meant," he said.

"Then you need to ask the questions you want the answers for."

"Are you in a relationship?"

I shook my head as my brows pulled together. What was going on that he would even think that? "I haven't been in a relationship since you left for Hong Kong."

He took a sip of his drink. I couldn't help but notice he didn't make faces or flinch at the alcohol. "Then explain to me why I saw you with a little boy at the playground in Oak Park last weekend."

My stomach dropped. I picked up my drink and threw half of it back. I spluttered and coughed against the strong drink. "What the hell were you doing in Oak Park?"

I never should have taken him to Oak Park. I never should have showed him that house. I picked that house because it was my favorite house in Chicago. I picked it to show him, because on the days I wanted to dream about a better life for me and Leo, I would walk a little bit out of my way so that I could see that house. By showing Kyle my dream house in a moment of pique, I'd somehow managed to let him see his son.

22

KYLE

"This is going to sound stupid," I admitted.

"It can't sound any stupider than anything you said to me so far tonight," she said with a sneer.

"I wanted to take a better look at the houses in the neighborhood you showed me. I was feeling… nostalgic."

"You're right. That does sound stupid. You decided to take a walk in Oak Park, and you think you saw me with some kid. You could have just asked me about it instead of jumping to conclusions."

I put my drink down and looked at her. I let my gaze linger on her features and her form. She was exceptional.

"Look at you, Clarissa. Why wouldn't you be married with a kid by now?"

She let out a bitter laugh. "You could have just asked me instead of jumping to conclusions."

"What am I supposed to think when I see you in a nice neighborhood playing with a kid?" I asked.

It was my turn to shrug. "I really don't know, Kyle. But why did you automatically jump to my being in a relationship? You didn't ask if I was babysitting or if the kid was my nephew. Why on earth would you think I was in a relationship with somebody else after I spent the night with you?"

I finished the drink with a single long gulp. "You're not in a relationship. You're not married. You're not divorced. Then who is the kid, Clarissa?"

She looked shocked.

After letting this eat me up for a week, she was right. I needed to be asking different questions. I wanted to know who the kid was and why she was in the park playing with him.

As I waited for her answer, that voice in the back of my head reminded me, *and this is why I wasn't supposed to be fooling around with the intern again*. Not only was it not professional and completely inappropriate, but she also tied my insides up to the point where I couldn't think straight.

It wasn't any of my business who she saw or if she had kids. The second I took her back into my life and into my bed, I needed to know everything there was about her. Not knowing something this major ruined my entire week.

She stared at the unfinished drink in front of her. Having seen how she reacted the first couple of sips, I figured she was contemplating whether it was worth finishing the drink or not. Surprisingly enough, she picked it up and tossed it back. Her entire body quaked, and she made the most unattractive grimace as she clearly did not enjoy the drink. She nodded at my drink. "You might want another one of those before I tell you anything."

I waved down the bartender

"Give me another one of these. Do you want anything?" I asked Clarissa.

She shook her head. "Can I just get a Coke?"

"Rum and Coke?" the bartender asked.

She shook her head. "Just Coke."

"Coming right up."

She drew squiggles in the condensation on the bar surface while we waited for our drinks. As soon as mine was in front of me, she nodded at it. "Drink up."

"What gives?" I asked as I set the drink down after taking a sip.

She took a few long breaths in through her nose before letting them out. She let out a soft moan on a sigh. It was almost a whimper. "I'm not seeing anybody," she repeated, "because I have a kid."

I stared at her as she wrapped her lips around her straw and took a long sip of her pop.

"Okay," I said. "Why didn't you tell me about him? Why keep him a secret?"

I wasn't going to judge her for having a kid. But I didn't understand.

She set her drink down and began playing with the corner of the napkin it was on. "I didn't tell you about him because I didn't want you to judge me too harshly."

"Is he why you didn't finish school?" I asked.

She nodded.

"What about his father? Is he around to help out?"

She turned and looked me directly in the eyes. "No," she said. "At the time, he was in Hong Kong."

She stared at me for a long moment.

"What a coincidence. I was in Hong Kong."

She continued to stare at me for a long time. I wasn't putting two and two together.

"I was in Hong Kong," I repeated.

She nodded slowly.

"You're telling me that I'm the boy's father?"

She continued to nod.

I set my drink down and stood up. "That's a very interesting story, Clarissa, but I'm not inclined to accept it."

"And why's that?" she asked.

"Because it just seems convenient. Don't you think so?" I pulled my wallet out of my back pocket, pulled out my credit card, and held it up for the bartender. "I think we're done here."

"So, that's it? We're done. We're over. You're just going to laugh in my face and walk away?"

"No one's laughing, Clarissa. This isn't funny."

"Then why do you think I'm joking?" she asked.

The bartender took my credit card. "The lady's, too?" he asked.

I nodded.

"If the boy is my son, why didn't you say anything before?"

Her eyes burned into me with a fierce glare. "You left without saying goodbye."

Was she ever going to let me get past that?

"I was planning on telling you, but then you were gone. And I didn't think having Alayna send you an email, '*Oh, by the way, you knocked up the intern,*' was a very good idea."

"You could have reached out to me at any point in time, Clarissa. How old is he? Four?"

"Don't you know how math works?" she asked. "He's five and a half. He started kindergarten this fall, and he knows how to read."

I had a son, and he knew how to read. It didn't seem real. Couldn't be.

The bartender set down the card along with the receipt to sign and a pen. I was still standing there trying to figure out what Clarissa wanted from me. She hadn't told me about my son when she first got pregnant, and she was only now telling me about him because I saw them together.

I scribbled my signature and put too much of a tip down before throwing the pen onto the bar.

"I've been back for months now, and you haven't said anything."

"You're right. I haven't. Would you have believed me if I had said something the first time you walked into James's office? 'Oh, hi. Remember me? You got me pregnant.' You didn't even know who I was, Kyle. You didn't even recognize me. What was I supposed to do?"

I didn't have an answer for her.

"I thought I meant nothing to you. And if that was the case, then we were all just better off with you not knowing about Leo."

"His name is Leo?" I sat back down on the barstool. Knowing my son's name somehow made it all the more real. "Leo? Is that short for anything?"

Clarissa shrugged. "Does it matter?"

"Of course it matters. Why would you name the kid Leo Love?"

"His name isn't Leo Love. It's Leonard Matthews."

I shook my head to clear my thoughts. Matthews? "My name isn't on the birth certificate?"

"Why would I put your name on the birth certificate?" she asked.

"Because I'm the father!"

"Now you believe me?"

"Clarissa," I growled and ran my hand through my hair. "Matthews, Matthews." I mumbled the name a few times. I could not place it, didn't recognize who I knew with that name.

I looked up. My brain was so muddled by everything, I hadn't fully recognized it as Clarissa's last name. I was being a dumb fuck. No wonder she hadn't told me I was going to be a father.

"I want to meet him," I said.

"I don't think that's a good idea," she said.

"And why not?" I leaned in. "If he's my child, I want to meet him."

"Because I don't want him getting confused."

"Do you bring so many men into your life that he wouldn't know one from another?"

She shot a glare at me that would have cut if looks could kill.

"No, I don't date. I don't see random men. He knows he doesn't have a father, but he's never asked me about you. The last thing I want to do is have you come into his life and treat him the way you treated me."

"I treated you very well."

She gave me a bitter smile. "If you treated me so well, why are we arguing about your five-year-old son whom you've never met?"

"How can you be so certain he's mine?" I snarled.

"How many people do you think I was sleeping with, Kyle?"

I shook my head. "I don't know, Clarissa. How many? You tell me."

"Your ego really does get in the way of your being able to think clearly, doesn't it?" She closed her eyes and shook her head before she seemed to shut down and get quiet. "If you're leaving, just go ahead and leave." She turned away from me, taking another long sip of her drink. I think she was crying.

"What is that supposed to mean?" I asked.

She lifted her hand to her forehead like she was getting a headache.

"Do I really need to spell it out for you, Kyle? Maybe I do, since you clearly don't even know how to count to five. I was a virgin when we met, and you're the only man I've ever slept with. So yeah, I'm pretty sure my little boy, who has the same blue eyes as you do, is your son."

23

CLARISSA

I was in a foul mood when I got home. It was a good thing that Leo was already in bed.

"How did it go?" Marci asked.

"Don't ask," I grumbled.

"That bad?"

"He doesn't believe me. I cried. I have been crying the entire walk home. Meeting him tonight was such a bad idea."

Marci frowned in sympathy with my bad mood. She unfolded from her spot on the couch and wrapped her arms around me in a comforting hug.

"He doesn't believe that Leo is his son." I sniffled.

"You told him about Leo?" she asked.

I pressed my palms against my temple, trying to push my head back together. "This is so fucked up, Marci. No, I didn't tell him about Leo. He saw us at the park. He's been angry with me all week. He came to Oak Park and saw us."

"I thought you said he lived in the Gold Coast area. What was he doing in Oak Park? Is he following you?"

I shook my head. "He had some half-assed excuse for being in the neighborhood. As far as I know, he still doesn't know where I live. But I showed him the house."

"Not your dream house?" She sounded so disappointed in me. "Why did you show him your dream house?"

"I was stupid and angry. He was playing games at work, thought he was being clever by making me take him on an architectural tour of Chicago again. So, I showed him the house. I wanted him to look beyond the façade, to see that there are more interesting things in the world than something with a famous name."

"You wanted him to see that there were more interesting things in you," she said.

I groaned and sank onto the couch. "Oh, God, it was a metaphor for our relationship."

"What are you talking about?"

I waved my hand about, dismissing my stupidity. Or maybe I was wafting it about. "Stupid stuff I said when I was trying to be profound and smart and witty, and furious and pissed off at him. I wanted him to regret what he did. I wanted him to regret leaving me all those years ago."

"Only it backfired and bit you in the butt."

I laughed. "It bit me hard. I probably have teeth marks."

She laughed. "What happened? Tell me."

I told her everything that I managed to understand through my confusion. Kyle saw Leo and me and jumped to the conclusion that I was married or had a boyfriend or a situation of some kind. I thought

I was going to play it off and deny everything, but I caved and confessed that Leo was his son and he didn't believe me.

"Leo isn't proof enough for him?"

I shook my head and held my hands out wide. "His name isn't on the birth certificate. Kyle seems to think that's proof that I'm trying to trick him or something."

"Get a paternity test," Marci suggested.

"Are those expensive?"

She shook her head. "I don't know. Not one of those genealogy tests. Those are expensive. You should be able to get a paternity test from the drugstore."

"And what? He pees on a stick and they match?"

"You're funny, Clarissa, even when you're stressed. I don't know how it works. But if he wants proof that Leo is his kid, he's going to have to agree to a paternity test."

"I don't want it to hurt Leo," I said. "You know, needles and drawing blood."

Her thumbs were already speeding over the front of her phone. Knowing Marci, she was getting answers for me in real time. She switched to swiping her finger across the device a couple of times, nodded, and then held her phone out to me. "See, it's do it yourself. A cheek swab, and we should be able to get it at the drugstore. There are no needles at all."

"What am I supposed to tell Leo?"

"Leo doesn't even have to know what's happening," Marci said.

"You know him. He's going to ask questions."

"Leo doesn't have to know anything. He's five. You tell them you're doing a science experiment or something."

I could handle that. Leo loved science.

The next day while out running errands, I purchased the same kit that Marci had shown me from her phone. Getting the test was the easy part. Asking Kyle to take it was a different matter.

On Monday morning, my nerves left me a complete mess. I had the box, ready to hand the paternity test over to Kyle the second he walked in the door. Only he didn't. I didn't find out for a couple of hours that he and James had a client meeting.

They returned some time later while I was helping Michelle fix an issue with the printer. For some reason, her computer decided to stop communicating over the network to the printer. This was an issue we had managed to troubleshoot before. It took the two of us yelling back and forth across the office to let each other know whether a document was sent or received.

When I was running back and forth between Michelle's office and the printer, I noticed that Kyle had come back, and he was set up in the conference room. Once we successfully managed to have a document print, I went to see him.

"I have something for you," I said before he could say anything.

"An apology?" he asked.

I shook my head. I didn't see how I owed him one. "A paternity test. You said you wanted proof, and this is the only sure way to provide that for you."

He grunted. What else had he expected?

"No," he finally said. "I want to see him."

Did Kyle think he could look at Leo and suddenly tell if he was the father? Would he recognize himself in the face of our little boy?

"Are you still interested in meeting him?"

"I am," Kyle said. His expression was blank, and I couldn't tell if he was upset or tired or both.

"Would you be interested in meeting us at the Field Museum this weekend?" I asked.

He shrugged.

"I don't know how to give you proof if you don't want to take the paternity test. I can't go back in time and somehow tell you before you left. If you want to meet him, you need to take the paternity test."

"I'll meet him first," he demanded.

"I have to package your part of the test with Leo's cheek swab and send it in together. If you meet us at the museum, you can do your cheek swab in the bathroom there."

"It's a cheek swab?" he asked.

I nodded.

He narrowed his eyes at me before nodding in agreement. "That should work."

"Good. Leo is not going to know what that test is for. If he asks me, I'm telling him it's a science experiment. And I would really appreciate it if you wouldn't say anything to him until we have results. Or until you are comfortable accepting that you're his father *and* that you're planning on being around."

He started to say something but stopped. "Can we call a truce, then?"

I nodded and bit my lip. Tears stung my eyes.

"Being this angry is exhausting. And I don't want to be angry at you, Clarissa."

"I don't want you to be angry at me either," I admitted.

Saturday morning couldn't come soon enough. Leo thought it was great fun to be part of a science experiment.

I rubbed a cotton swab along the inside his cheek and sealed it in a test tube and put the box in my bag. As a reward, I promised him a morning at the Field Museum of Natural Science. It was always a treat because he loved the dinosaurs so much.

Kyle stood just inside the main entrance, waiting for us.

Leo got a little shy and crowded in close when I started talking to Kyle.

"Leo, this is one of Mommy's friends. He wanted to come see the museum too, so I invited him."

Leo nodded but didn't seem too interested in meeting Kyle.

Kyle squatted down so that he didn't tower over the two of us. His eyes went wide when he saw Leo clearly. He had to see that Leo looked like a miniature version of himself, the same dark hair, the same blue eyes. And the same stubborn streak.

"My name is Kyle. I understand you are an expert on dinosaurs. Your mom thought you might be able to help me learn something new."

Leo eased away from my side slightly.

Kyle continued to ask Leo questions until Leo nodded.

Kyle stood. "You have something for me?" He said it like it was some kind of a drug deal. I rolled my eyes and retrieved the box out of my bag.

"This is your part." I handed him the test.

"Once you've completed your part, I'll send everything in."

"You expect me to trust that you'll not tamper with the test?"

My gut twisted. I thought he didn't want to be angry with me any longer. But clearly, he was.

"I have his part with me. I'll put it in the box first, and then you can put your part in the box. I'll even let you seal it, and we can go drop it in a FedEx box together." I had put a lot of thought into how to proceed. I didn't want him to find a way to worm his way out of taking the test.

24

KYLE

The Field Museum of Natural History was a very different experience when viewed through the eyes of a five-year-old. We stood and stared at the Tyrannosaurus Rex skeleton for I don't know how long. I was ready to move on and look at anything else, but Leo was still completely fascinated and refused to budge.

"He loves dinosaurs," Clarissa repeated. She had warned me at least five times in the past ten minutes.

This was going to be a long morning.

As we continued through the museum, every new exhibit was his favorite. He had so much information about each and every dinosaur skull we looked at.

"And this one is Mommy's favorite," Leo said as we stopped in front of the triceratops.

I looked over at his mother.

She had a soft smile on her face. "He loves dinosaurs," she said again. This time, I caught the hint of exasperation in her tone.

"I see that," I replied.

Apparently, he also really loved everything about this museum—dinosaurs, rocks, gemstones, mammal exhibits. What I thought was going to be a few hours extended longer and longer. By mid-afternoon, Leo was exhausted and asleep against my shoulder. I carried him as we headed toward the exit.

"Thank you," Clarissa said. "This was a good day."

"I had a good time," I said, completely forgetting that I was supposed to be angry at her, forgetting that I doubted the little boy asleep in my arms could have been my child.

How different would things have been if I had known?

Leo made a noise and squirmed a little bit in his sleep. I gently patted his back.

"I can take him if he's getting too heavy," Clarissa said, reaching toward the boy.

"He's fine. He doesn't weigh a thing." And even if he did, at that moment, I didn't think I could have put him down. I felt it in my core that this child was my son, and she hadn't been trying to pull one over on me. "What now?" I asked.

"Normally, we'd go outside, and I'd let him run around in the park until he wore himself out." She gestured at him. "He's already out. If it were nicer, I'd suggest we sit outside and let him nap in the sunshine."

But it was not a nice day outside. It was one of those cold, wet fall days where the chill of winter threatened an early arrival.

"I guess I'll just take him home and put him to bed. He'll probably wake up before we get there, and then we'll just have a quiet evening watching movies."

"So, that's it?" I asked.

She shrugged. "Some days, he can go and go and go. And those days can be very exhausting. And others, he runs out of steam a whole lot earlier in the day. I think he was so excited to have someone to show all of his favorite things to, he just got overwhelmed."

"You could come over to my place and we could have dinner," I suggested.

She narrowed her gaze at me. "Are you sure that is really a good idea?"

She seemed skittish, and I didn't blame her. After all, we had been arguing mere days earlier.

"I've been to your place," she started. "It's not particularly child friendly. I don't know if Leo would be able to contain himself the way you might expect him to."

I let out a long breath. She had a very good point.

"I could follow you home, and we could have dinner somewhere in your neighborhood," I suggested.

"Are you trying to find out where I live?" she teased. Her eyes lit up as a smile danced across her expression.

"I'm saying I've had a very good day, and I don't think I'm ready for it to be over," I admitted. "I'd like to spend more time with you and with Leo."

"Really?" she asked. "Even without having completed the paternity test?"

I shrugged. She was right. It seemed like an out of character request, especially after I demanded proof that this was my son.

We stared at each other for a long moment.

She rested her hand on my arm. "I'll tell you what," she started. "I have no idea how sleepy or cranky he's going to be when he wakes up. Why don't I take him home and give him a chance to finish resting, and then we can meet somewhere for dinner?"

"You really don't want me to know where you live, do you?" I asked.

She shrugged me off. "There are some things I need to keep private," she admitted. "You never were interested in where I lived before."

"That's because you had a roommate," I said.

She shook her head. "I still have a roommate"—she ran her hand down the sleeping boy's back— "and he's five. We would love to have dinner with you, Kyle, but we'll meet you somewhere. Okay?" After a long moment, I realized this was probably for the best.

"How are you planning on getting home?"

"Same way we got here. We'll take the train."

"No, he's asleep. Let me call you a car, and promise you'll meet me for dinner."

"There's a great little Greek place that Leo really likes. How about we meet there?" She told me where it was, and I agreed.

I carried Leo as we walked outside and waited for her ride to show up.

She reached out and took Leo from me. She seemed to buckle under his weight. While he felt so small in my arms, he looked like a huge kid when she carried him.

"Let me know that you've gotten home safe," I said before I closed the car door and they drove off.

I watched the car drive off with Clarissa and my son. If there was ever going to be a future for us, I was going to have to put in a bigger effort. I shoved my hand in my pocket before I headed off to the train and found the paternity test.

I played with the box as I waited for the train in the station. I tossed it around and read the instructions. Everything was fairly clear, and I could have swabbed my cheek while sitting on the train. No one around me would have even noticed.

However, I did wait to complete it until I was in the privacy of my own home. I swabbed my cheek and stuck the extra-long Q-tip into a little vial and shoved it back into my pocket. I kept it on me so that I would remember to give it to Clarissa at dinner.

My phone pinged with a text message. It was Clarissa.

Made it back. Leo woke up on the way home. Told him about dinner, and he already plans on bringing his favorite dinosaur model to show you. Be prepared.

The kid is going to grow up and be a paleontologist, I texted back.

It didn't take her long to respond. *That wouldn't be so bad. But I think he really wants to design enclosures for dinosaurs at theme parks. He still thinks that the dinosaur zoo from the movie is real and I'm just being mean by not taking him.*

I will be thoroughly impressed when he shows me his toys. Promise, I responded.

See you at seven for dinner. I felt ridiculously happy to read her last message.

The few hours I had to kill before dinner felt like an eternity. I made it to the restaurant early, only to learn that Clarissa and Leo had also arrived early.

Leo spent his time telling me about dinosaurs and telling me about his day at the museum, even though I had to remind him that I had been there with him. This didn't seem to make a difference. My discussion with Clarissa was mostly about Leo.

"It was like magic. He went from not being able to read. He recognized his ABCs, but words were beyond him. And then less than a week later, he could read almost any word he got his eyes on." Pride shone through her eyes. "He's a smart kid."

"That reminds me." I reached into my pocket and handed over the vial with my cheek swab.

Leo reached out and grabbed it. "Are you doing the science experiment too?" He sounded very excited.

Clarissa extricated my sample from his fingers. "Yes, he is doing the experiment too. Now give me that. That's not yours. What have I told you about grabby hands?"

She opened her oversized purse and pulled out the mailer box that came with the kit. She looked me dead in the eye and said, "You're seeing this, right?" As she put the plastic tube into the box, she tilted it so that I could see that there were only two plastic tubes. She pulled one out, showing me that it was imprinted with the word *Child* on the side.

I nodded and watched her as she sealed the box.

She held it out to me. "Do you want to put it in the mail or should I?"

"I'll trust you to handle it from here," I said. "What are your plans after dinner?"

She narrowed her gaze at me. "I take him home and I put him to bed."

"Alone?" I asked.

She nodded. "Alone."

"What would you say if I invited you and Leo out to the country next weekend?"

"Sounds like it could be interesting. It could also be very cold," she said.

"I think the weather next weekend is supposed to be nicer than this week. We could go find one of those corn mazes. That's something Leo would like. They still have those, don't they?"

Clarissa laughed. "I have no idea. I thought those were only in horror movies."

"Not at all. I think it's just something they do with large fields of corn after they've picked everything. It could be fun."

"What, were you thinking about getting a cabin or just driving up for the day?"

"I could get a vacation house," I said. "We can make a whole weekend of it. It'll be fun. Come on."

"Can we, Mommy? I want to see a corn maze," Leo said. It was good to have the kid on my side.

She let out a sigh. "Well, if the two of you are going to gang up on me, I guess I should say yes."

25

CLARISSA

Maybe I should have let Kyle meet Leo sooner. After all, everything seemed to have changed after that one morning at the museum. Even though I sent the paternity test in, I felt like maybe Kyle was going to come around and say he didn't need the test results to believe that he was Leo's father.

After all, couldn't Kyle simply look at our little boy and see that he was a mini copy of himself? I know I saw it every time I looked into Leo's blue eyes. I had all the proof I needed.

I still wouldn't let Kyle know where I lived, even though he was taking us out to the country.

"Come on, Clarissa. I have to pick you up."

"No, you don't. Leo and I will grab an Uber, and we can leave from your place."

"It would be easier on everybody if I just came to you," he argued back.

We were still arguing almost every day, but the reasons were less important. I don't know if I would even call our exchanges arguing. It was more like we were bickering like an old married couple. Maybe we were past the flirting stage of our relationship and into something deeper where differences were a matter of course. We accepted them, discussed, and continued moving forward.

"Just tell me where you live. I won't judge. It'd be easier if I just picked you up at your apartment."

I wasn't going to let him know just how close he had come that day. I didn't want him to know, not yet.

Kyle rolled his eyes at my refusal, but I was going to hold that one small bit of privacy as close as I could.

"How about, instead, you bring our bags to work in the morning? And then we can pick Leo up from school after work on Friday?" he suggested.

"We can't do that. Leo would be too tired and too cranky. We all will be too tired and cranky after a week at school and work. I would have to carry everything into work with me, and everyone would know that we were going away for the weekend together."

He grunted. "At least let me pick you up on Saturday morning."

I shook my head. "Saturday morning, Leo and I will be at your place bright and early with our bags all packed and ready to go. Think of it as saving you from having to drive through city traffic to come get us."

Kyle grunted in acquiescence. I knew he didn't like the plan, but it's what was going to happen. All Friday night, Leo was bouncing off the walls. He was so excited and ready to go. Maybe I should have let Kyle pick us up, but I had to be honest with myself. I didn't know how I was going to handle being alone with him with Leo in tow.

I didn't know what a family vacation with the three of us was going to be like. Was Kyle going to expect me to sleep with him? Would I even be able to, knowing that our son was in the next room over?

It was just as well that I had insisted we show up at Kyle's place on Saturday morning. He wasn't even ready to leave. At least he was dressed.

The drive out of the city didn't take long, and we didn't go too far north into Wisconsin before he navigated to a quaint little lake house.

Once out of the car, Leo immediately ran for the shoreline.

"It's too cold to get into the water," I shouted out after him.

Fortunately, he seemed to understand that we weren't here to go swimming. He picked up a rock and threw it into the lake. He seemed to think that was great fun. While Kyle and I unpacked the car, Leo walked up and down the water's edge tossing stones into the water as if he was returning them to where they belonged.

Without much of a plan other than to find one of these mysterious corn mazes, we didn't do too much more than drive around the countryside, looking at a lot of cows and stopping to eat when we found a place for lunch.

"I'm beginning to wonder," I announced as we sat in a booth at the small diner waiting for our lunch, "if these corn mazes actually exist."

So far, we hadn't stumbled across one as we randomly drove around, getting lost in the countryside.

"There has to be one around here somewhere," Kyle said.

"You folks not from around here, are you?" our waitress asked when she set down our drinks.

I smiled and shook my head. "We're up from the city."

"I want to see a corn maze," Leo announced.

Kyle gestured across the table at him. "What he said. You don't happen to know of any around here?"

"Oh, there are plenty of those around. What you want to do is find an apple orchard or one of those farmers' markets. Most of them might already have shut down their mazes for the winter, but I bet if you jumped on one of your smartphones, you could find something. I'll be right back with your food."

"Thank you," I said as I pulled out my phone and began trying to find something close.

I laughed. "Well, this says the world's largest corn maze is actually back the way we came from."

I showed Kyle the map on my phone.

"There's gotta be something closer by." I scrolled through and found another location. "The trick is going to be finding a place that still realizes it's fall and isn't trying to get ready for Christmas."

"Christmas is months away," Kyle said.

I shook my head. "It's a lot closer than you think."

We made note of a couple of places that looked like they would be within driving distance from where we were. By the end of the day, I still didn't believe corn mazes existed outside of movies. But we did end up at a petting farm where Leo had the time of his life running around and petting baby cows, llamas, and goats.

Leo was exhausted by the time we got back to our cabin by the lake. He was almost too tired to take a bath before he got in his pajamas. There were tears, and not just from the overly exhausted little boy.

"Why don't you just let him go to bed?" Kyle asked at some point in the middle of the wrestling match between Leo and me.

"Because he smells like a goat," I pointed out. "I try not to let my little boy go to bed smelling like a goat. Once Leo was in bed, and after I read him a bedtime story, I made my way back out to the small living room where Kyle was.

"Would you like some wine?"

"Is that the best idea?" I asked.

"We could skip the wine and we could go to bed." Kyle stepped in close and ran his hand along the side of my hip.

My heart began hammering in my chest. It was hard to catch my breath. My nerves did that tap dance routine they always did when Kyle got close to me. I glanced over my shoulder toward Leo's room.

"I don't know if I can," I said, uncertain whether I could be with Kyle while he still wouldn't admit that Leo was his son. I wasn't going to have proof on the paternity test at least for another week.

Kyle noticed my hesitation and stepped away from me, leaving me alone and cold.

"Don't worry, Clarissa. I'll sleep on the couch tonight."

The way Kyle joked with me on our drive back into the city the following day gave me hope that he wasn't too angry over our sleeping arrangement.

I wanted us to be a family. I knew we couldn't be together until I knew that Kyle trusted me. And as much fun as I had with him and Leo over the weekend searching the Wisconsin countryside for a corn maze, he still hadn't said anything to me acknowledging or accepting that he was Leo's father. Maybe I needed to take the first step? Maybe I needed to show Kyle that I trusted him by admitting to Leo that Kyle just wasn't one of Mommy's friends, but he was actually Leo's father.

The thought nagged at me for days. I didn't get a chance to speak with Kyle alone at the office like I wanted to. So, even while we both sat in the conference room, reviewing final floor plans for the upstairs remodel at work, I sent him a text message.

Can we meet on Saturday?

Kyle glanced at his phone and then lifted his eyes, meeting mine from across the room. He gave me a slight nod.

My phone buzzed in my hands.

What's wrong with after work tonight?

Picking up Leo from daycare, I responded.

We could all go to dinner, Kyle texted back.

I want grownup talk without little ears.

Won't little ears be with us on Saturday? he asked.

I'll get Marci to babysit.

Can you stay out late? Kyle texted.

I bit my lip and tried to suppress my natural inclination to blush. *I'll have to ask, but I'm sure Marci would be offended if I didn't.*

Sounds like a date.

As always, when it came to dealing with Kyle, my nerves were a complete mess. I really hoped to have the paternity results by then. I wanted us to get past this whole proof thing so we could be together.

26

KYLE

I had dinner with Clarissa on Saturday night. In her typical fashion, I had to meet her at the restaurant. I let her pick it, as usual. And as usual, I wondered if we were in an area close to where she lived or if she purposefully chose restaurants far from her home just to deflect and confuse me.

"You look lovely tonight," I said as she stepped into a restaurant.

It was another family friendly kind of place. It made sense. Why would she choose small, romantic places that would be good for a date when in the past five years, if she was eating out at a restaurant, it would be at a place that was good with kids?

"Thank you." It surprised me how she was still capable of blushing when I complimented her.

"You wanted to meet with me." I reminded her that this was her idea.

I honestly hoped that she was going to have the test results. I was anxious to set the uncertainty behind me. Even though there were times that I was convinced that Leo was my child, I didn't necessarily trust that gut feeling.

We followed the hostess to our table. Clarissa ordered a glass of wine. If she was drinking, that probably meant she was nervous.

"Is everything okay?" I asked after the waitress left with our order.

Clarissa played with her fingers and bit her lip. "I was thinking… I was wondering…" She started and stopped a few more times. "What do you think if I let Leo know that you're his father?"

I sat up a little straighter. My heart beat a little faster. "Did the test results finally come in?" I asked.

She shook her head. "They haven't come in yet. I don't know what's going on. I've reached out to the company, but they weren't able to provide me with any tracking information, so I haven't gotten anything yet."

"But you're willing to tell Leo I'm his father without that confirmation?" I asked.

She pinched her face, pursing her lips and drawing her eyebrows together in a grimace. "I'm not the one worried about the paternity test results. I *know* you're Leo's father."

I sat back and cleared my throat. "I don't know, Clarissa. Do you think it's really the best idea? I don't think it's a good idea, at least not until you've received the test results."

She continued looking down at her hands. "I thought we were getting along so much better."

"Our getting along has nothing to do with your setting Leo up for disappointment. What are you going to tell him if those test results come back and show that I'm not the father?"

She started to laugh.

I couldn't see what was so funny.

"I don't understand why you're being like this, Kyle. I know you're the father. Just because you need the proof doesn't change that."

"If you don't need the proof to tell him, then why have you waited so long?"

"Because he's five," she said with an intensity that I didn't expect. "You weren't around for him to know. He likes you, Kyle. It would be really great for him to also know that you are his father."

"I don't think I can do that right now, Clarissa. Not with everything that's going on with work."

"What is that supposed to mean?" she asked. "I thought your takeover from the Stone Group was going smoothly. Hasn't the ownership already transferred? James seems to have already shifted into his senior consultant phase."

"The transition is going well. I haven't taken over complete ownership just yet. I have clients with my international office that I feel are falling behind. I have clients that need my attention, and I can't focus on their needs if I'm being distracted by this situation with you and Leo."

"Are you saying we're a distraction now?"

I let out a long breath. She was upset. That wasn't my intention.

"No, you're not listening to me, Clarissa."

"I am definitely listening. However, I don't think you're aware of the words you're using."

"Maybe not. Maybe this was a mistake," I snapped.

She folded the napkin from her lap and set it on the table next to her full glass of wine.

"Mistake? Me? Dinner? Or finding out that you had a son and getting to know him?"

I couldn't answer her. It all felt like a mistake. Letting her back in my life had been a rookie move.

I should have known better, but there was just something about her. I would always be drawn to her no matter where we were. She was a flame, and I was a fucking helpless moth when it came to being attracted to her light.

"I see," she said.

I didn't know what she was responding to because I hadn't said anything. Maybe that was her problem. I wasn't talking.

"I think we're done here, Kyle. I will make sure to get you those test results as soon as they come in. Thank you for the wine. I think it's best if this evening ends now."

I stayed there, completely numb and unresponsive, as she walked away. How could she be so decisive?

I paid our waitress for our drinks and tipped her heavily for the inconvenience of taking over a table during dinner hours without actually ordering a meal.

At home, unable to relax, I decided to check in with the Hong Kong office. Was there anything interesting going on that might need my attention? Typically, this information would come to me through Alayna, but at the moment, I didn't see how getting her involved would be helpful.

I didn't expect anything to come from my email since Hong Kong was thirteen hours ahead of Chicago, and it was Sunday morning their time.

But I did get a response from Sullivan, who was the head of that office. That had me curious. I sent another quick message. *Are you open to a video call?* The video call that I assumed would only take a few moments lasted several hours. And by the end of it, I knew what I had to do next.

Monday morning, instead of going to the office, I contacted Alayna directly to have her coordinate my travel schedule, and then I followed up with James to make sure that he could continue working with the local clients while I needed to go do some serious hand holding of several clients in Hong Kong.

By that evening, I was on a flight from Chicago to Hong Kong. By the time the plane was over the Pacific, I was second-guessing my real motivation.

I had just left Clarissa and Leo behind again without saying anything. I had to accept that there might not be a way back from this. Clarissa was already having a hard time forgiving me for the first time I left her.

I lost a complete day to travel and didn't feel the necessity to hurry along to my hotel once I arrived in Hong Kong. I knew I should get some sleep because in the morning, I had to be in the local office as a functional presence to help belay the fears of a client for a smaller project. Instead, while still at the airport, I found a lounge with a bar. I needed a drink to take the edge off everything that I felt was coming at me.

"You look like you've had a very long flight," an older businessman said after I dropped my carry-on bag to the floor and let gravity pull me down onto a barstool.

I simply nodded with an affirmative grunt, not in the mood for conversation.

"I know that feeling too." He already had a drink in front of him and took a sip from it. "It's always so much harder when you feel like you've left a mess at home."

For a moment, I stared at him bleary eyed. Jet lag was catching up to me fast. "What is that supposed to mean?" I asked.

"Traveling like this for work, it always seems harder when it feels like I'm running away from a problem at home. Half of all meetings can be taken care of with a conference call, a video meeting, or an email anymore these days. I guess I'm just getting tired of sitting in an airplane only to realize that I could have spent the past fourteen hours fixing whatever it was my wife has been bitching at me about. And now I've gone and left her with the same problem, forcing her to either live with the issue until I get back or she has to find a way to take care of it on her own."

"Sounds like you have a situation on your hands," I said.

"I was willing to fly halfway around the world to solve some problem like a hero, but I left my wife stuck with something I should have already fixed. We run away so we can play hero for somebody else when the person we need to be a hero for the most is the one we just leave behind." He threw his drink back, draining it completely before getting up and leaving.

I stared after him. Did he have problems at home? Or did he somehow know that I had walked away from Clarissa yet again?

27

CLARISSA

I didn't see him all the next week. When Kyle didn't come into the office again on Monday after not being around, I expected it was because he had more client meetings I wasn't aware of. I knew he could get busy and forget to reply to texts. I tried to not take it personally, even though I really did. I knew things would be fine once I saw him again, so I tried not to think anything of it. And I didn't, not until later that morning when James called everyone into the conference room.

"Clarissa, I need you to join us," he said as he tapped on my desk.

"My backup receptionist isn't here until after lunch."

James made an affirmative noise in his throat, nodded, turned around, and crossed the small lobby area before locking the front door. "It's not like we're expecting anyone to come, and the phones can go to voicemail."

"Okay," I said a little nervously as I followed him to the conference room.

When I got there, I expected everyone to be gathered around the table looking over the final plans for the upstairs remodel. Everything had been signed off on, and building was underway. The plans were to not knock a hole in James's current office until his upstairs office was finished. I automatically assumed this impromptu meeting was about the timeline for that.

"Okay, everyone," James started. "As everyone knows, we are officially becoming the Chicago office for the Kyle Love Firm."

I cast my gaze around the conference room. Everybody Kyle had brought in, Steve, Nick, and Alayna, were all there. Kyle was the only person missing.

"Shouldn't Kyle be here for this?" I blurted out without even thinking.

"That's what I'm here to talk to you about," James said with an expression I thought might be a touch of disappointment. "Kyle has decided to relocate, at least temporarily, back to Hong Kong. I will be staying in the office a little bit longer than originally contracted for while he manages a situation overseas."

I shot Alayna with a hard glare. She knew and she hadn't said anything. She grimaced and looked away. I knew in my gut that grimace wasn't meant for me.

"He didn't say anything to me about that," Steve said.

Alayna cleared her throat, and everybody turned their attention to her. "It's my understanding that something came up rather suddenly. His original plan was to only be there for a few days last week. Apparently, the situation requires his attention on a more full-time basis," she said.

My stomach plummeted. I couldn't tell if I was breathing or not. I knew he hadn't been around, but no one had said anything about his being out of the country. This was somehow worse than the first time he had taken off without saying goodbye.

After all, this time, he knew he had a son. He knew how much it had hurt me when he chose to leave before. My immediate discomfort was rapidly replaced by a fiery ball in the center of my chest. I was incandescent with rage. I sucked in a breath and held it, preventing myself from screaming.

"Are you okay, Clarissa?" Alayna asked.

I pasted a smile across my face, not expecting to fool anybody but needing to fool myself. "I'm fine. Sorry, you were saying?" I gesture back at James to continue whatever it was he needed to say. By that point, I could no longer hear words, just the roaring and pounding of my pulse in my ears.

I sat there and stared at the wall over James's shoulder as he continued to give what I could only think might've been a pep-talk about how the office would continue to function under the Kyle Love brand regardless of his presence. I didn't hear the words, and I didn't really pay attention. It wasn't until everybody was leaving the room and Steve stopped and patted me on the shoulder that I realized the meeting was over.

I startled, looking up at him. "I'm sorry?" I asked, aware that I missed what he had said.

"I said it's just like the last time, isn't it?" he said.

"What's like the last time?" I asked. I was so stuck in my own head, I hadn't noticed that Steve looked almost lost.

"Kyle taking off for the other side of the world just as we're about to reach the end of a project," Steve explained.

"Oh, yeah, that." I let out a half-chuckle. I didn't see anything remotely humorous in the situation, but if I didn't laugh and joke about it now while I was at work, I was in danger of curling up on myself in a ball of crying mess. "You're the one who works for him. I would think this would be something you have to get used to."

"Yeah, I think he really pissed Alayna off this time," Steve said before leaving.

I was the last one to leave the conference room. I walked in a daze right past the crowded office that Alayna and Jenna shared.

"Clarissa," Alayna called out.

I might have heard her. I might've thought it was all a bad dream. I didn't stop until I reached the receptionist desk.

Alayna was right behind me. "Clarissa," she said again.

I looked at her and blinked a couple of times. I didn't know what she wanted of me or what I wanted her to say. There was nothing that she could say that could fix this situation. Besides, no one here was supposed to know there was even a situation that needed to be fixed.

"I just wanted to let you know that I didn't know there was anything between the two of you when he left for Hong Kong six years ago."

"Who says there's anything going on between us now?" I asked.

"I know the two of you are trying to keep it quiet. I'm not dumb, but Kyle is crap at keeping secrets," she said.

"This sudden need to be in Hong Kong seems to be a bit of a secret. Don't you think?" I asked.

"I seriously doubt he knew that he wanted to go to Hong Kong until he was on a plane and halfway there. There are some things he just doesn't think through," she said.

"But you figured there's something going on between us now?"

"I've had my suspicions, but it wasn't until I saw the two of you arguing that I actually worked it out. I just wanted to let you know I'm sorry he's being like this to you."

"Sure," I said. "He's such a great guy otherwise, right?" I didn't try to keep the disappointment or sarcasm out of my voice.

"He can be a real jerk," she admitted. "He's always been so good to everyone who works for him. I didn't think he would be like this to someone he cared about."

I laughed again, that bitter, derisive burst of air that held no mirth but prevented me from screaming. "Clearly, he doesn't care about me. If he did, he would have said something a week ago about going out of town. I would have found out from him, not from James, and not from you, that he had plans for not sticking around."

"I hope this doesn't change your decision to continue working with us," Alayna said.

"What does that mean?" I asked.

"I'm aware that you're finished with classes soon and that you anticipate interning here for another semester. You're good at what you do, and we are lucky to have you."

I stared at her for a long moment. "Did James put you up to that?" I asked.

Alayna shook her head. "That's my own opinion."

"Thank you," I mumbled.

At that moment, I hadn't even considered what I would do next. All I knew was right then, I needed to shove all thoughts of Kyle Love out of my mind and focus on what I needed to do. I had a course to finish. I had an internship to finish. I had a little boy to take care of.

I stared at the wall just beyond Alayna.

"I think I need to take the rest of the day off. If you could let James know. I'm sorry, but I just can't be here right now," I said.

She nodded. "I understand. I'll let him know. Take all the time you need," she said.

"I don't have the luxury of letting this take too long," I said as I gathered my things. "I'm not in a position to run away to the other side of the planet every time things get a little complicated."

I unlocked the front door and stepped outside. The early winter wind was freezing and cut through my unbuttoned coat. It somehow felt appropriate after the bad news I had just gotten. I walked to the station and texted Marci while I sat on the train ride home.

I need you to get Leo this afternoon, and can you keep him for the night? I typed out. It was hard to see my phone through the blur of tears.

Did Kyle come back? Are you celebrating? She texted, followed by an eggplant and a peach emoji.

He left me again.

The fucking coward, where is he? Do you need me to beat him up for you?

I smiled weakly at her fierce protection over me. I never would have survived the last time he left if it wasn't for her. It didn't seem fair that she was the one to have to take care of me again.

He ran away to Hong Kong again.

That bastard. Don't worry about Leo. I'll take care of him. Are you okay she asked.

I'm going to get drunk and cry myself to sleep as soon as I get home.

I will check on you tonight to make sure you're still breathing, but I'll keep Leo with me and Davey, she texted.

Thank you. I owe you so much. I sent the text to Marci and then stared at my phone for the entire train ride home. There was nothing keeping me from texting Kyle. Only, for some reason, I couldn't.

He hadn't bothered to reach out to me once in the past week to let me know he had left, so why was it my responsibility to ask him why he left me again?

28

KYLE

Six weeks later.

It was raining. It had been raining for weeks now. I stood and looked out over the skyline of the city that had been my home for six years. The city that I thought I had left behind once I returned to Chicago. Fireworks illuminated the sky in the distance in a festive explosion of color and celebration of welcoming in a new year.

I wasn't feeling particularly festive. I could have been at a party drinking champagne. Instead, I was alone in a cold apartment, aware that other people were having fun while I was alone due to my own stupid decisions.

If I were in Chicago, I could've been wearing warm pajamas. And they would be matching the pajamas that Clarissa and Leo also had on. Because she would do something like that. Understanding that Clarissa needed her private space, I would have invited them over to spend the new year with me, or I would have gotten that little lake house again where we could have celebrated like a cozy little family.

I could have spent Christmas with them. I could've made a snowman with Leo. I could have gotten Clarissa something really nice because she deserved nice things. Only, I wasn't there, and I was fairly certain she no longer wanted to have anything to do with me.

This was a shitty way to end the year. Only a couple of hours earlier had I truly realized how much I'd messed up.

In the time since I left Chicago, Alayna had chewed me out more than once for having abandoned the Chicago office while it was in its infancy. But tonight, she let me have it for having left Clarissa.

"I can't believe you did this to her twice, Kyle." Alayna had never been furious with me in all the time she had worked for me. She had only ever gotten truly angry with me a few times. She had even put up with relocating to Hong Kong for several years before putting her foot down and demanding to return to Chicago. Even then, it hadn't occurred to me that she would quit being my assistant.

"I don't know what she has told you—" I started to defend myself.

"Shut up and listen to me, "Alayna demanded. "You've broken something in her. She hasn't said anything, but it is clear she is struggling. Did you even bother to send her a congratulations when she completed her coursework and was allowed to graduate early?"

"I thought you would take care of that," I admitted.

"Of course, I took care of that from the office, but that's not what I'm asking. I'm asking if you personally have reached out to her at all?"

"I haven't," I admitted.

"I hope you find comfort in your steel beams and glass walls because if this is how you treat someone who clearly cares about you, you don't deserve any better." She hung up on me.

"What the hell is that supposed to mean?" I yelled into empty space.

My phone immediately pinged with a text from Alayna. I expected her to say that there was interference on the phone or some technical reason the call ended. The text said, *See your email.*

I opened my laptop and launched the email program. There was one from Alayna waiting for me. It was titled *Chicago Office Updates*. I opened the email, wondering why Alayna was still at work before my brain caught up with the fact that it was still just before lunchtime in Chicago and people would still be working even though it was the last day of the year.

I began reading.

Here is a quick update regarding the Chicago office situation. The stairs are in, and the remodel should be completed in the next few weeks. Phillip and Steve are a phenomenal team and work well with James and with clients. Nick has given notice and is transferring to a firm in New York. Also, I quit.

I immediately tried to call her back.

"I take it you read my email?" she asked immediately upon answering the phone.

"Alayna, you can't quit," I begged.

"You can't pay me enough to continue to work for someone with the basic lack of empathy you have exhibited toward Clarissa."

"You're quitting because of the intern?" I practically snarled.

"No, I'm quitting because of the way you have treated somebody who clearly loves you. You can't be bothered to break up with her in person. You just left her."

"She needs to get over that mistake. It was years ago," I said.

"I'm not talking about whatever happened between the two of you before, Kyle. I'm talking about what happened less than two months ago. I see her almost every day, and she knows that I talk to you. I'm stuck knowing that you won't talk to her. I can't do this anymore."

"You can't do what?"

"Support someone who is so callous. We had a good run, but it is time for me to move on."

"What am I supposed to do without you?" I asked.

"I suggest you try to get your shit together and your priorities in order. I am leaving all of the client contact information and pertinent files in the competent hands of Jenna. She'll be in touch at the start of the year to find out whom she should transfer information to while you are in Hong Kong. I doubt she'll be as flexible as I have been." She spoke so evenly, so clearly, like she always did.

"Alayna, you can't."

"I can, Kyle, and I have. Today's my last day in the office, and it's my last day working for you."

"But, Alayna." She couldn't abandon me like this.

"Say goodbye, Kyle."

I let out a heavy breath and realized that one simple mistake had ramifications in a much broader scope than I could've ever guessed. "Goodbye, Alayna," I said, realizing I had screwed myself on so many levels.

"Goodbye, Kyle."

I stared at the phone in my hand and started to think of how I could fix this. Alayna was a decisive woman, and I knew that her quitting was not something she would lightly change her mind on. However, I wasn't the absolute asshole she thought I was being. Or was I?

I needed to go back to Chicago. I needed to face my fears and confess to Clarissa that having a son was something I had never expected, and even after I met him and knew in my heart that he was mine, I had to stay firm on my convictions and see proof before I could admit it Clarissa.

Clarissa had been right. I only needed to look at Leo and see that he had my eyes. Would I be able to convince Clarissa that I was truly sorry? That I had been wrong?

As the fireworks continued lighting up the night sky, I returned to my laptop and struggled with the purchase of an international flight from Hong Kong to Chicago. I missed Alayna already. I was so used to calling her and having her make all of my travel arrangements. I barely knew what I was looking at as I selected a flight.

I immediately called Sullivan.

"Happy New Year!" he shouted into the phone.

I could hear cheering and general noises coming from his end of the call. "I'm going to need you to take over the Greenway project," I started.

"What are you saying? I can hardly hear you," he continued to shout into his phone.

"I need you to—" I started again.

"Whoa, whoa. Why does this sound like work?" he asked.

"I am trying to tell you something," I said.

"Unless you're calling to tell me happy New Year, whatever you have to say can wait until we're back in the office."

"It can't wait," I said.

"Why not?" he asked.

"Because I'm not coming back to the office. I'm getting on a plane for the States. You'll have to take over for the project." I was yelling into the phone at this point.

"So I'm back in charge of the project I was in charge of before you showed up?" he asked.

"Something like that," I said.

"Fine, whatever. Email me the details. I'm too drunk and in too good of a mood to want to figure out what you're trying to tell me. I'll see you in the office next week."

It wasn't until then that I noticed he was slurring his words slightly. Five minutes after midnight on the first day of the year was probably not the best time to be making rash business decisions, but I had already purchased my plane ticket.

"No, you won't. You'll get an email. I will talk to you later." I ended the call.

I had approximately four days to pack everything up and get myself to the airport. It wasn't until that point that I realized I wasn't even certain about whom to contact regarding the short-term lease on this apartment. I doubted that I could get out of whatever agreement I was financially committed to. I would just have to accept that as my idiot tax because mistakes I made in my relationships were now costing me money. They already cost me my personal assistant, and they most likely cost me my son and the woman I was in love with.

"Damn it." I threw the phone. I was in love with Clarissa, and I had fucked everything up. I needed to get back to her.

I didn't even know if there was somebody living in my place in Chicago. Alayna said she was giving everything to Jenna. I didn't have a phone number for Jenna. I guess all of the details would have to be worked out and finalized once I got back.

29

CLARISSA

The drizzle of rain was cold, and the sky was overcast and gray. Everyone around me complained of the cold, but to me, it was practically balmy, especially without the cutting wind coming in off Lake Michigan.

Seattle had been an unexpected gift, and even after a week here, I was loving it. I didn't have a job yet, but I was hopeful, and I was getting interviews for junior architect positions.

I had been wallowing in misery in Chicago, coming to grips with the fact that I could no longer put my life on hold waiting for Kyle. He would come back to Chicago eventually, but that didn't mean I needed to be there waiting for him.

A few weeks after James made his announcement that Kyle had left for Hong Kong, I decided I could no longer continue to work for Kyle Love's firm, even if it was James doing the work.

I made the decision to also leave Chicago. I didn't know at the time where I was going to go, but I needed to make it happen.

"I hate to see you leave, but I understand. I have some friends at your school. Let me see if I can pull some strings," James said when I finally got up the nerve to talk to him about it.

I know that I had James's connections with someone in the department to thank for applying all of my work history at the Stone Group toward my internship credit hours. I was able to graduate without having to complete another semester's worth of interning.

At some point in mid-December, I had thought that Kyle would have reached out because I finally received the paternity test results. He should have gotten his copy of the results at the same time. I didn't need to read them to know what they said. My nerves still fluttered in anticipation of receiving a text or a call from Kyle admitting he was wrong. That never happened.

Everything in my life felt like it was leading up to the worst Christmas I would have in years. I felt so alone on Christmas morning while Leo excitedly opened his presents from Santa Claus. I was too depressed to have remembered to put a package under the tree for me. Fortunately, Leo was too distracted by all of his new toys to have noticed that Mommy didn't have anything to open.

We were still in our pajamas when Marci and Davey came over for brunch. Since they lived in the same building, they came over in their pajamas too.

"I brought a hot dish," Marci announced as I opened the door.

"I thought you were making cinnamon rolls. I made sausage balls and hash browns," I said.

"I'm making the cinnamon rolls," Davey announced. "I just need your oven to finish them. That way, everything smells nice and festive."

I let them bustle about in my small kitchen while I set up TV trays and made the champagne mimosas for us to drink. Leo kept getting into the middle of the kitchen trying to show off his new toys.

"Baby, you can show Aunt Marci your new dinosaurs when she is done. There's not enough room in the kitchen for you and your dinosaurs," I said as I guided him out of the kitchen yet again.

"Why don't you help me find a good Christmas movie to put on to watch while we wait for breakfast?" I asked him.

This had Leo distracted for maybe fifteen minutes, and then he was back in the kitchen trying to tell Davey about how Santa ate the cookies we left out and he had the crumbs to prove it.

I don't know what it is about fashion that women's clothing can't have pockets, but little boys' pajama pants can. He reached into his pocket and pulled out a handful of cookie crumbs.

"Leo, you do not have cookies in your pockets," I exclaimed.

"I only have the crumbs that Santa left." He showed me more crumbs that he pulled from the other pocket.

"Oh, baby, you can't keep cookies in your pajama pockets. Come here." I pulled him next to a garbage can and wrestled his pockets inside out and began brushing off the rest of the cookie crumbs that were sticking to the flannel fabric.

Leo whined. "But Mommy, that's my proof that Santa was here."

I pointed to the Christmas tree. "Isn't that enough proof for you?"

After the cookie in pocket debacle, I got him to settle down until Marci and Davey were ready with the food.

Marci handed me an envelope. "Merry Christmas," she said.

I set the envelope down and pointed to a box under the tree. "Leo, will you bring that to me for Aunt Marci?"

He got up and dragged the heavy box to Marci and Davey. "This is from Leo and me," I said.

"You open yours first," Marci told me.

I opened the envelope. Inside was a festive Christmas greeting card, a crisp hundred-dollar bill, a folded-up sheet of paper, and the printout of an ultrasound.

I stared at the image for what felt like forever before an excited squeal left my mouth. "Oh, my God, how did you ever keep this secret from me? You're gonna have a baby!"

I got up and immediately hugged her and then hugged Davey. "You guys are going to make the best parents. Congratulations!" I looked at the unopened gift that sat on the floor between them. "You might want to leave that here. I can get you something else," I said.

Marci turned her attention to the box. "What do you mean?" she asked as she ripped open the top to a small case of wine. "Oh, yeah, I'm not drinking for a couple of months."

"Right," I said.

"But that's not everything." Marci pointed at the card.

"What are you talking about?" I asked as I pulled out a folded printout of a flight itinerary and an address in Seattle. "You're moving?" I asked. Christmas was dissolving around me, and I started to cry.

"Don't cry," Marci said as she wrapped her arms around me. "Look." She rattled the printout with travel arrangements on it at me.

"With the kid on the way, we thought it would be better to be close to my family," Davey started.

"But what about Marci's family?" I asked.

"Marci doesn't have contact with anyone in her family," Davey pointed out.

"I'm her family," I practically shouted.

"You are," Marci said. "That's why we want you to come with us." She shook the paper again.

"What do you mean?" I asked.

"You said it yourself, there's nothing keeping you here any longer, and you've always thought about maybe moving to the Pacific Northwest. This is a perfect opportunity. Come to Seattle with us."

I finally looked at the paper she was pushing at me. It was plane tickets to Seattle for me and Leo. My jaw dropped open. I stared at her, and then I stared at Leo. I couldn't say that my job was keeping me here because it wasn't, and the only people who would have kept me in Chicago were now moving.

"I'd have to get a job," I said numbly.

"You have to get a job anyway," Marci pointed out.

I looked around our small apartment. "We'd have to pack everything up."

"We're getting a moving truck in a couple of weeks. You can just add your stuff to it."

"Are you serious?" I asked.

"Marci wouldn't agree to move if she didn't think that you would be able to come also," Davey said. "I know better than to try to split the two of you up."

"I already have a job starting just after the first of the year," Marci said.

"But what about your job?" I asked Davey.

"I have something lined up to start at the end of January."

"What about a place to live? Do they have old neighborhoods like this?" I asked.

"We were really hoping you would say yes because we've already rented a house with more than enough room for you and Leo," Marci said.

"Wait, you want us to live with you?"

"We are already over at each other's places all the time, and this way, we can help each other out. I was hoping you would be willing to help with the baby," Marci said.

"Of course I am willing to help with the baby. Yes, oh, my God, yes!" There was no reason to stay here. I'd have to find a new school for Leo, but he was young enough that it wouldn't be a problem. All I needed to do was give notice for the apartment and find a job in Seattle.

What I thought was going to be an uneventful and sad Christmas had turned out to be one of the best Christmases ever. I was given a chance at a new life.

The week following was a blur of activity. The landlord was feeling generous and only charged me for one more month if I could be out by January first because there was a waiting list for the building. We moved everything into Marci and Davey's place in a matter of days, and on the second day of January, Marci, Leo, and I were on a plane relocating to Seattle. Leo didn't miss a bit of school since I managed to get him registered before the term started.

30

KYLE

I more than half expected to see Clarissa when I stepped into the office. Instead, I saw Jenna looking rather frazzled, speaking with some woman I didn't know.

"What are you doing here? she said as she looked up and saw me.

"This is my office," I said.

"James—"

"I'm going there now." I cut her off as I breezed past her into the back of the office. I stopped when I got to the place where James's office should've been. Instead, I was face-to-face with a staircase headed up to the second floor.

"James's office has moved," Jenna said as she came behind me.

"I see that," I snapped out. I started to climb the stairs when she stopped me.

"Where are you going?"

I turned around. "To see James," I told her. "I'm getting tired of this little game. I'm clearly here to find out what has been going on in my absence, and I will be relying on James to provide me that information, thank you," I said, dismissing her.

"Nobody is upstairs," she said.

"What do you mean?" I had been under the impression from Alayna before she quit that the creatives, the architects, and drafts team had all moved their offices upstairs.

"Nobody's here," she repeated.

"You're here. Are you gonna tell me what's going on?"

"If you give me a chance. I'm in the middle of something, and then I can catch you up with anything that I know. Why don't you take a look at your new office space, and I'll be in as soon as I can?"

"I think this is something you need to fill me in on right now," I said.

Jenna let out an exasperated sigh and crossed her arms. "I get that you're used to snapping your fingers and having somebody jump to your needs, but I'm not your personal assistant right now. I'm in the middle of training somebody, and I need to at least show her how to answer the phone before I can walk away and have a chat with you."

I wasn't a fan of her tone. "Do you talk to James like this?" I asked.

"When he is being unreasonable, and right now, you are being unreasonable. If I had known to expect you, maybe I would have been a little more available. I'm only asking for maybe ten minutes."

"Fine, is my office at least in the same place?"

She actually rolled her eyes. "No, your office space is now in the area where Philip and Michelle had their working spaces. We didn't change anything from the last set of blueprints."

She returned to whatever it was she said she was doing. I guess she was training a receptionist. Which made sense considering Clarissa spent her afternoons being the department intern. If I recalled correctly, we had had some issues with keeping a temp in the afternoon receptionist position.

My new office had more square footage than I had ever worked with before. I remembered when we were designing it, feeling that sense of achievement in my career where I would finally have all the space I needed to not only work but display models and hold meetings in one place. The furniture looked sad and minimal as it was overwhelmed by the magnitude of the size of the office. I was going to have to talk to somebody about having some interior design work done as I dropped my briefcase on my desk. Who the hell would that be since Alayna quit?

I had just unpacked my laptop computer when Jenna walked in.

"I'm really surprised to see you here. I thought you were going to be in Hong Kong for a while," she said.

"Well, when Alayna notified me that Nick was leaving and that she quit, I figured maybe I needed to come back and do some damage control."

Jenna stood in the door to my office with her arms folded. She shook her head. "You might be a little too late for that. Alayna was very definite when she quit. She left me with a stack of files and contacts to go through, but I've barely had time to catch up."

"Why isn't there anybody here?" I asked.

"Technically, the office is closed for the week. Everybody has taken a few days of vacation. We weren't able to shut down the week between Christmas and the new year like James used to do because of the buyout and other business items that needed to be wrapped up before the end of the calendar year. We were all hands on deck putting in a lot of hours the week after Christmas, so he went ahead and closed for this week."

"Nobody told me that was happening," I complained.

"Well, nobody told me you were going to show up," she pointed out.

"But you're here," I mentioned.

"I'm here because it is my job to make sure the office is up and running. I've been interviewing and hiring a new receptionist and an additional office assistant so that when I take my two weeks at the end of the month and go to Jamaica, I know that phones are being answered, invoices are being sent, payroll has been managed, and projects are properly filed. We aren't in a position for me to have the luxury of taking off at the same time as everyone else just yet."

"Is it really so bad?" I asked.

"We've been hemorrhaging employees for a month. For a firm this small, it's that bad, and with Alayna gone, it's probably worse than that. She did the work of at least three people."

"Isn't James managing the clients properly?"

"James has been running this company for years. He's not the problem."

"Let me guess, you're going to say the problem is me," I quipped sarcastically.

"I'm not gonna say you're wrong." I did not miss the bitter tone in her voice.

"When you say hemorrhaging, other than Nick and Alayna, are we really so strapped?"

"Considering that Clarissa left as soon as she graduated, we're down thirty percent. When there's only ten of us to begin with, that's a heavy hit."

"What do you mean, Clarissa left?"

Jenna shrugged. "Just that. She got all of her employment time here applied to her internship hours, and she up and quit."

I just stared at her for a long moment. It was bad enough that I returned to Chicago and was unable to rely on Alayna to keep me updated. But now I found out that Clarissa had left the firm, and I came back in the middle of a week when everybody was gone…

"Did Clarissa leave her contact information?"

Jenna just shrugged again. "I have her employee files, if that's what you mean."

"That's exactly what I need. Can you get that for me?"

"Sure, but I don't see how it will do you any good, since apparently, she's also left Chicago."

My heart stopped beating in my chest. I couldn't wrap my mind around what Jenna was telling me.

Everything was going from bad to worse.

When Alayna called and chewed me out on New Year's Eve, she had failed to mention that Clarissa was gone from the firm, let alone from Chicago.

"Are you certain?"

"It's what I heard from James."

"Hasn't she given you her new address?" I asked.

"Not yet. She can pull her tax forms straight from the online service that takes care of payroll. It's not like I need to mail her anything."

"What about her last paycheck?" I asked.

Jenna huffed out a chuckle through her nose. "How much of your business did Alayna take care of for you? We haven't written checks here for a very long time. Everything is handled by online transfer of funds. We don't even write checks for the small things anymore. Everything gets auto billed through James's credit card. That way, he has plenty of points to use for travel."

"You have no way of contacting her?" I asked.

"As far as I know, her phone is still the same. You can always try to call or text her," she suggested.

"I don't know if I ever had her number," I lied. Clarissa had blocked me several weeks ago.

"Right, of course not," Jenna said with dripping sarcasm. She probably knew there was something going on between us just as Alayna had figured it out.

"Can you just bring me her file?"

With an eye roll and another shrug, Jenna turned and walked away. Within a few minutes, she returned with a file folder.

"This is all I've got," she said as she dropped a manilla file folder on my desk.

I sucked in a breath as I opened the file to learn more about Clarissa than she had ever told me herself. I laughed out loud when I read her address.

All this time, she had lived in Oak Park without telling me. I closed the file and carried it out, handing it back to Jenna as I left the office.

"I guess I'll come back in a couple of days when everyone has returned from their little vacation."

Jenna exposed her teeth to me more than smiled. "That would probably be best unless you have a project that requires peace and quiet."

I left my office uncertain how to proceed. I couldn't go home because there was a short-term rental in my place for another week or two. I found myself in Oak Park. Somehow, I was able to find that same house Clarissa had shown me back in the early fall. I ended up walking past her apartment building and realized it was only a block from the playground where I had first seen her with our son.

Their absence was an infinite void in my gut. I needed to find them. I needed to fix this.

31

CLARISSA

Starting a new job is always nerve-racking. It didn't help that Leo chose this morning, of all mornings, to not want to go to school.

"You liked school yesterday," I reminded him as I helped him to get his coat on.

He whimpered and whined through the whole process.

"I will be there to pick you up after daycare," I said.

"But I wanna stay with you," he said as I pulled his hat down around his ears.

"I want to stay with you too," I said, "but I have to go to work."

"You didn't have to go to work yesterday," he pointed out.

"That's because Mommy is starting a new job today. I didn't have that job yesterday."

"You can't play with me anymore?" I thought my baby boy was going to start crying. He was miserable. If he started, then we would both be late because I would have to stop everything and cuddle with him until he felt more secure. Leo didn't dissolve like that much anymore. He was getting to be such a big kid that sometimes, I forgot he was still only five.

I lowered down in a squat until I was at his level. "You know I love you more than anything."

He nodded and his lower lip quivered. He was breaking my heart.

"How about tonight when I pick you up, you and I go find a pizza place to bring home dinner for Aunt Marci? We can all have pizza for dinner."

He nodded without much enthusiasm. I knew his reluctance was for leaving me and going to school, but I couldn't help but think I felt the same way over the prospects of finding a decent pizza in Seattle. We had only been here a few weeks, but I was still in search of something that would remind me of all my years in Chicago and the exceptional pizza I could find anywhere in the city.

With much cajoling and promises of dinosaur movies in the middle of the week, I managed to get Leo out the door.

I was breathless when I arrived at the new office.

"Sorry I'm late," I said to my new manager and senior architect, Dominic. "My kid didn't want to go to school this morning."

"My kids never want to go to school. But they're in high school." He laughed. "How old is yours?"

"Leo is in kindergarten," I mentioned. "He only goes for a half-day and then he spends the rest of the day in childcare, unless his aunt picks him up early."

"Right, right, you moved out here with her? I seem to recall your saying something along those lines during the interview."

"Yes," I answered. "She and her husband (I didn't feel like going into the details of their relationship, especially since I knew that while

Marci was thrilled with being pregnant, she wasn't so thrilled that Davey wasn't putting a ring on her finger) transferred out here for his family. I decided it would be a good time to take the opportunity to also get out of town."

"Well, we are glad to have you. Okay, okay, this is your desk. IT is up on the fifth floor. Rosalie will take you upstairs to get you introduced and get you all of your computer logins."

It took a minute to remember who Rosalie was and where her office was located. I pointed back toward the front of the office space we were in. I had already met so many new people that names and faces were starting to blur.

"Right, right, she was that first office just beyond the receptionist desk on the first floor," Dominic confirmed.

I had never been in an architectural firm as large as this one. They even had their own IT department. It wasn't just the receptionist and the draftsperson left troubleshooting to make sure the plotting printers were connecting to computers.

After Dominic gave me a brief tour of where I'd be working, he left me on my own to find my way back to Rosalie's office.

"Think of it as trial by fire," he said jokingly when I accused him of pushing me into the deep end of the pool without even knowing if I could swim.

The hardest part of getting back to Rosalie's office was getting myself out of the maze of cubicles my workspace was in the middle of and to the elevator bank. Fortunately, Rosalie's office was close enough to the elevators on the first floor that I didn't get too lost. Besides, all the offices with doors had those glass walls, so I could see which one she was in.

I knocked on her door and she waved me in.

"Did that man abandon you?" she asked with a broad smile on her face.

"He did seem to take great pleasure in my panicked response when he told me I was on my own to get back here," I said.

"Dominic tries to be a hard ass, but he sucks at it. He's too nice." Her phone rang, and she laughed as she looked at it. "Speak of the devil." She answered the phone, and Dominic's voice filled her office.

"Has the new kid made it there yet?"

"She's sitting right here, and you're on speakerphone."

"Good, good, you didn't get lost. I knew you could make it," he said with his quirky double words.

"I managed to find my way here, no help to you," I said, jumping into the easy camaraderie that was in the office.

"Try not to scare her off, Rosalie. And have her back to me after lunch."

"Thanks for making my job easier." She laughed as she hung up the phone and turned her attention back to me. "We have paperwork for you to fill out, and we have to get your employee ID badge. Oh, and we need to make sure that you're set up with IT for computer and network access. Then we need to spend some time going over how we track billable hours."

I smiled to myself. I was going to have billable hours. I was so excited.

"Everything okay?" Rosalie asked.

I nodded. "It's just my first time having billable hours. It kind of feels like I made it, you know?"

"But you've been working in architectural firms, I thought," she said.

"Yeah, I spent the last few years as a receptionist for one while I finished up my degree. I pretty much helped around the office. I'm pro at getting the plotter back onto the network. Other than that, I've worked as an intern, and none of that is billable."

Rosalie nodded in understanding. "I admire your enthusiasm." She gestured in a circular motion with her hand before bringing all of her fingers together quickly. "Please keep that in mind when you are actually tracking your work. It is probably the one thing the creatives moan about the most."

I suppressed a giggle.

"Why don't we get started?" Rosalie stood up.

I followed her out of her office and into an empty room with some equipment. She walked me through the process of having a picture ID made. We waited around while my ID card was processed. It was still warm when she handed it to me.

"Don't lose that, it is also your key card." She began rummaging through a cupboard and pulled out a box of different colored lanyards. "You don't have to use one of these if you don't like them, but until you figure out what you want, these are handy. You need to keep your key card on you at all times."

As she started going over the specifics of working at Brennus Enterprises, my head started to fill up and all I could do was nod and hope I remembered all the details.

"How are you feeling about everything?" She checked in with me as we rode the elevator up to the IT department on the fifth floor. "Are you hanging in there? Okay?"

"It's a bit overwhelming. I hope there isn't a quiz at the end."

She laughed. "You're going to do just fine here. You aren't from this area originally, are you?" she asked.

I shook my head. "I recently moved here from Chicago."

"How do you like it so far?" she asked.

"So far, it's a lot warmer."

"That's just because it's winter. In the summer, you'll wish it was warmer. Do you have any questions for me so far?"

I let out a sigh and tried to think of anything reasonable and pertinent to ask. "I feel like a blank whiteboard and you're just beginning to leave notes on it. I'm sure I will have questions later, but right now, I'm just trying to keep up."

The elevator dinged, and the doors slid open.

"Now, don't let the folks in this department intimidate you. They can be a little surly and cranky, but they keep our computers up and running, so we all put up with it."

I followed her through another maze of cubicles.

"I thought of something I want to ask. I know this isn't necessarily job related," I started.

She looked over her shoulder at me. "Sure, what can I help you with?"

"Do you know a really good place for pizza?" I asked.

"We have a place called Windy City Pizza, and they have that deep dish style from Chicago. I can't tell you how it compares since I've never actually had Chicago style pizza in Chicago."

"That sounds like a good place to start," I confessed. "I'll let you know how it is in the morning. I promised my son we'd have pizza for dinner, and so far, all we've found are the chain stores that aren't exactly the best, are they?"

32

KYLE

I was still aggravated that Alayna had quit on me. I let that anger supersede the pain I felt over having lost Clarissa. I spent the next few days wandering around Chicago, unable to get comfortable in my hotel room. I wanted my home, and I wanted my family.

However, the only thing I was guaranteed was that once the short-term rental was ended, I would be able to move back into my own place. I had no idea if I would ever be able to get Clarissa and our little family back.

I didn't know what to do with myself, unable to focus and feeling lost in the city I considered my home territory.

It wasn't until James came back to the office after his brief holiday that I felt like I was making any headway in my life. I stood in his new office, impressed with how completed it appeared. In contrast, my office looked like it hadn't been moved into yet.

"I'm surprised you didn't ask me where Alayna went," he said after I barged in and barely said hello before I demanded he tell me if he knew where Clarissa had relocated to.

"I know where Alayna lives," I said. "She reminded me of it constantly the two years I managed to keep her in Hong Kong. If I needed to track her down, I know where to look. I doubt I would be welcome if I showed up on her doorstep."

James chuckled. "She did seem pretty ticked off with you when she let me know she was done working for you. I even tried to hire her for myself, but she said would have nothing to do with this firm anymore."

"She certainly didn't hold back when she was letting me know that she quit. Alayna hadn't told me that Clarissa left, and I need to find her. All I have is her old address in Oak Park and a blocked phone number."

"I can't give you her new address because I don't have it. I don't even think she has a new job yet, but I can tell you she's in Seattle," he said.

"Seattle?" I asked.

"I'll call you when I get there," I said as I turned and walked out of his office as soon as he confirmed. I went straight to my hotel. I packed up my bags and headed for the airport.

I had been through the Seattle airport plenty of times on my way to Hong Kong before, but I had never actually stopped in the city for a visit. I found a hotel and got settled in before I contacted James to see if he had any updates.

"I don't, but I can give you a list of contacts I shared with Clarissa. Maybe you can track her down through one of those firms," he suggested.

"That sounds like a good place to start," I told him. I spent the next week acting like some kind of private investigator, calling architecture firms to find out if they had any new hires. And if they did, was Clarissa now working for them? When I realized no one would tell me if there was someone with her name working there, I began calling the reception desk and asking to speak with her, hoping the receptionist would simply put my call through.

I don't know how many days it was before it worked. The call went to Clarissa's voicemail. I didn't realize how badly I missed her until I heard the recording of her sweet voice telling me she'd get right back to me.

I hung up the phone immediately and got a car to her office.

I didn't know what to expect when I approached her. Would she be happy to see me or not?

"Clarissa," I said quietly as I stood behind her.

She swiveled around in her chair and looked at me. Her expression switched from one of shock to anger to being absolutely neutral and blank. "What are you doing here?" she asked in sharp, clipped tones.

"I need to speak with you," I said.

"Are you serious?" she snapped.

"Oh, my God, are you Kyle Love? Clarissa, what is Kyle Love doing in your cubicle?" A man about my age with dark hair asked.

I noticed Clarissa pasted a smile on for him, but she didn't even have a glimmer of joy when she looked at me.

"Yes, Dominic, this is Kyle Love. I interned for him."

Dominic seemed rather enthusiastic to meet me when he shook my hand. "It's a real pleasure to meet you. I'm a big fan of your work. Sparkman Tower in Doha is a work of genius."

"Thank you. I always like hearing that my work is appreciated." The Sparkman Tower was the design that put my name on the map of renowned international architectural design.

"Are you staying in Seattle for any length of time?" he asked.

"I really don't know," I answered.

"Sure, sure, well if you are and you're available, I'd love to buy you a drink and pick your brain sometime."

"We'll see how this trip goes. If not, maybe next time. Clarissa, do you have a moment to discuss this?" I asked, hoping she would pick up on the hint that we needed to talk.

She turned to Dominic. "Do you mind? Is there a conference room we could borrow or…?"

"Why don't you take a coffee break and go get some of Seattle's finest? Have your little chat outside the office," Dominic offered.

"Thanks." She turned and picked up her coat and then pushed me to begin walking away. She did not say anything as we trailed through the cubicle farm where she worked and back down the elevators and outside.

"What are you doing here, Kyle?" she snapped.

"I came to find you and Leo," I said.

"Why?" I could feel the resentment coming from her.

"Because we're a family."

She started laughing. "So now we're a family? How long did it take after you got the paternity test results to decide we're a family?"

"Don't be like that, Clarissa. The test results don't matter," I said.

She walked with a brisk pace through the spitting cold rain. She stopped, turned to face me, made some noise halfway between a grunt and a growl, and then began walking again. I followed but only managed to get a few steps in before she stopped and turned on me again.

"I don't understand. You've had the test results for weeks and you're only now coming to talk to me about wanting to be a family. I don't think so. You should have believed me from the beginning." She stormed off.

"I haven't gotten any test results, Clarissa," I called out after her. "I realize I have been a fool. I don't need some DNA test to tell me that Leo is my son or that I love you."

She charged back toward me. Her eyes were narrowed as she shot a deadly glare at me. "You certainly need something, because if you really did love me, you wouldn't have left for Hong Kong again without saying anything to me for a *second* time."

"I get it, Clarissa. I fucked up," I admitted.

"You can say that again," she snarled.

"Did you know that Alayna quit working for me?"

Clarissa stopped walking again. "I had no idea. I thought she was too smart to always put up with your shit, but you did admit that you overpaid her. What did you do to finally drive her away?"

"She said that in the end, it was because of how I treated you," I admitted.

Angry tears that I had mistaken for raindrops ran down Clarissa's cheeks.

"It took Alayna quitting for you to realize that you missed me? That's really rich. You couldn't have missed me for my own sake? You couldn't have believed me when I confessed that I've only ever had a relationship with you and Leo was your son. Why not? Why couldn't you have just missed me and done the right thing without Alayna kicking you in the butt?"

She was right. It took my losing Alayna to realize I had lost absolutely everything.

I looked up and saw the coffee shop on the corner.

"Let me buy you a coffee and we can talk about this," I said.

Clarissa passed back-and-forth at the corner as we waited for the light to turn. We made it about halfway across the street before she stopped.

"You know what, Kyle? Buy yourself a damned cup of coffee. I'm done. I have to go back to work." She turned around and left me standing in the middle of the street.

I just stared after her, unsure of what to do, until the cars wanting to drive started honking their horns at me. I started to run after her but was cut off by a speeding truck that nearly hit me. I retreated to the coffee shop and over a hot mocha began formulating my next steps. I had relied too much on Alayna for managing my professional life. So much so that I hadn't really been managing my private life at all. Everything needed to change.

I needed to prove to Clarissa that she could trust me and that we belonged together.

33

CLARISSA

"**D**avey sent a package," Marci announced as she walked into the kitchen of our new shared house. She had a large, padded envelope in her hands.

"Hopefully, it's not all the bills that didn't get paid when we left," I teased. I didn't look up as I washed dishes in the sink.

She tossed the large package onto the table.

"Is that for me?" Leo asked as he came bouncing into the room.

"No, sweetie," I said. "That's for Aunt Marci. Davey sent it from Chicago."

"When is Uncle Davey gonna get here?" Leo asked.

"Not soon enough," Marci complained.

It was the last week of January and Davey still hadn't left Chicago yet. He was supposed to put all of our belongings onto a moving truck and head out here, but something came up and he had to extend his stay in Chicago by a couple of weeks. It was making Marci nuts. We were all living out of suitcases and folding lawn furniture because all our real tables and chairs and couches were crammed into their old apartment. Leo and I shared an air mattress while we waited for our beds to arrive.

"Come here, Leo," Marci said. "Help me open this up. Maybe it is something fun."

Leo climbed up on a chair so that he could reach the table more easily.

"What do you think it is?" Marci asked as she shook the package.

Davey had been forwarding any mail that came to the old address every week. This was probably just another envelope of that even though it was much bigger than what he typically sent.

"Maybe it's a flat dinosaur," I said jokingly. I turned away from the dishes and leaned against the front of the sink so I could see what the goodies inside the package were.

"Mommy," Leo complained. He could have told me exactly why a dinosaur couldn't have fit in that envelope. At least he was beginning to understand when I was being silly.

He tore open the package with the enthusiasm of ripping into presents on Christmas morning. Marci helped him pour out the contents. There was a bunch of bills that hadn't been properly forwarded, a small envelope that looked like a card with Marci's name scrolled across the front in Davey's handwriting, and a large paper board envelope.

"What's this?" Leo asked as he lunged for the large paperboard envelope.

"What does it say?" Marci prompted.

He was getting so good at reading that we were constantly encouraging him to read everything. He studied the envelope for a long time

"Why is this number crossed out?" he asked Marci. He pointed to different words on the front of the envelope. "That says return to sender on the yellow sticker, and that says love, and that's Mommy's name."

"What? Let me see, please?" I tried not to rush across the small space and snatch the envelope from Leo's hands. "This was sent to Kyle, but it looks like it was returned to the lab." I picked at the multiple address labels on the front.

"Holy crap, is that the…" Marci twisted her face, trying to find the right words she could say in front of Leo. It wasn't like we could actually spell anything out around him anymore.

I bit my lip and started nodding like some kind of bobble head.

"Yeah, I'm pretty sure that's what this is."

"But what is it?" Leo asked.

I shot Marci a panicked look. She swooped in and grabbed Leo and began tickling his ribs.

"I think it's boring work stuff," she said as she swung him around before setting him on his feet.

Leo giggled and ran out of the kitchen.

"What are you gonna do?" Marci asked.

I had no idea. I was holding the test results for Kyle and Leo's paternity test. This had to be the copy that was supposed to have been delivered to Kyle.

"This probably explains why he told me he didn't get his test results," I said.

"And why it took them so long to get your copy sent to you." Marci finished the thought for me. "Maybe going with the cheap drugstore test wasn't the best idea."

"Maybe not." I shrugged. "But it's what we did."

Marci raised her brows and stared at me. I knew she wanted me to say something, but I honestly wasn't sure what to do. My insides felt like indecisive, panicked goo.

"I think I'll finish the dishes and maybe when that's done, I'll have a better clue about what to do about this." I shook the envelope.

"Let me know if I need to run interference with the kiddo," Marci said.

"Right now, I can't even process all of this," I admitted.

I tried to let my mind go blank while I finished the dishes and cleaned the kitchen. I hoped that I could somehow reach a state of decision-making clarity and Zen. By the time I was done, I was just as confused as before. I let out a long, slow breath as I sank onto a chair and stared at the envelope from the paternity testing place. I didn't need to open it because I knew what it said. However, this was meant for Kyle, and he didn't know conclusively that he was Leo's father. Making a decision, I stood up and found Marci and Leo on the couch watching TV.

"I'm going to take a walk. Are you good here?" I asked.

Leo didn't look up, but Marci gave me the thumbs-up signal. "I've got my phone. Just let me know if you're going to be late," she said.

I grabbed my phone and put on a jacket before heading out the door. I was getting used to the weather here. While it wasn't very nice out, overcast and cold, it was still better than the snow and wind back in Chicago. I didn't walk very far before I pulled out my phone and unblocked Kyle's phone number.

I stared at it for far too long. I didn't know if I could handle talking to him. I started to text him, but the words would not come out right.

Finally, I texted. *Are you still in Seattle?*

Yes, I'm still here, he responded almost immediately.

My throat went dry, and it was hard to swallow.

Are you willing to meet me this evening? I held my breath as I hit the *Send* button.

Where and when?

The house we were renting was only a few blocks from a busy street with a coffee shop on the corner. I texted Marci that I was going to meet Kyle in a few minutes to discuss the contents of the envelope in my hands.

Are you sure? she asked.

I responded, *No, I'm not. But I need to do this.*

As I walked the few blocks to the coffee shop, I texted Kyle the crossroads and told him I would be waiting there, inside.

The coffee shop was warm, and the smells of coffee and baked goods soothed my jangled nerves. There was something very cozy and comfortable about the setting. Hopefully, that would support my needs as I had to face down all my fears in the form of Kyle Love.

I was there for maybe fifteen minutes before he came crashing into the coffee shop.

"Clarissa," he said as he approached me. "Is everything all right?"

I couldn't say anything. My tongue felt thick and sticky in my mouth. I held out the envelope to him. "Here. I don't know what happened. It looks like they sent your test results, but they were returned. I guess they tried to send them to me."

He took the envelope from me and stared at it.

"It looks like these have gone on a bit of an adventure." He chuckled.

I didn't know how he could find humor in the situation. Then again, I had a habit of laughing when I really wanted to scream.

He let out a long, drawn-out breath. I understood how he must have felt. After all, he wouldn't be able to claim that Leo wasn't his after he read the documents inside.

"Thank you, but I told you I don't need these." He ripped the envelope in half, crossed the café, and then shoved the two halves into the garbage before returning to stand in front of me.

"I told you, I know that Leo is my son."

"It certainly would have been easier if you had believed me the first time, Kyle. I'm getting tired of having to repeat myself with you. This has been so stressful, and I don't know what to say to you anymore." I swiped at tears that escaped and ran down my cheeks.

He slowly sank to his knees before he took my hands and held them.

"You can say you forgive me. You can say you'll give me a second chance. You can say…"

"You left us," I said in the pause of his words.

"And I was so very wrong to have done so. I won't do it again."

"But you did it twice. How can I trust you?"

"Give me the chance to earn back your trust," he practically begged.

I pulled my hands out of his and stood up. He stared up at me from his position, still on the floor.

"That's a lot to ask," I said.

"Will you at least think about it?" he asked.

I bit my lip and nodded. "I'll think about it," I said before I left the café and walked home.

34

KYLE

I watched Clarissa leave the coffee shop. I had a lot of work to do to earn back her trust, but I saw into her eyes when she handed me the paternity test results. From what I saw there, I could tell she still wanted me to be there for her son, even though she never said the words. She still loved me. If she didn't, she wouldn't be hurting so badly.

I knew I would do anything for her because this pain in my core could only be because of how much I loved her.

I had to settle in Seattle. I needed to find a place to live. In the meantime, I still had an architectural firm to run without a personal assistant.

As tempted as I was to book a flight and be in Chicago on Monday morning, I knew I needed to stay around in case Clarissa texted me. I needed to prove to her that I was good to my word and that I would be sticking around.

I had to wait for Monday when I could give Jenna a call in the office. She refused to give me her personal phone number, which was probably just as well. She liked to remind me that she wasn't my personal assistant and that I couldn't pay her enough to take on that job.

"How difficult is it to set up an interview for an assistant?" I asked the second Jenna answered the phone.

"Good morning to you too. I just walked in the office. I thought you were in Seattle, or are you back in town?"

"No, I'm still in Seattle," I said.

"Then shouldn't you still be asleep or something?" she asked. "I literally just walked in the office. Give me a second."

I waited for a brief moment, listening to the sleepy hold music.

"Okay," she said when she came back to the line. "What is it you need help with?"

"Who do you use to hire an assistant?" I asked.

She hemmed and hawed a bit before coming up with an answer. "I guess I would put together an ad for one of those job search boards."

"You don't just contact some agency and have them send somebody over?" I asked. "That's what Alayna always did."

"I don't have the same connections or resources that she has. I'm not some kind of super assistant. I run a business office. I juggle bookkeeping and personnel and that kind of work. It's not the same thing."

I grunted a harumph.

"How did you find Alayna and hire her to begin with?" Jenna asked.

"Truth?"

"Yes," she said.

"I poached her from a competitor years ago," I admitted. "At the time, I had thought it was a surprisingly easy thing to do. Later, I discovered it was because I paid her twice her current salary."

"Why does that not surprise me?"

"So I'm on my own when it comes to hiring a new assistant?"

"Yes, you are. I mean, I can place a listing for you, but you need to come up with the job skills you are looking for."

"Do you think that information might have been in the files Alayna left you?"

"That's always a possibility," she started. "I haven't had time to go through everything. Some are physical files. Others are on the computer."

"When you say some are physical, what are we talking about, a file folder or two?" I asked.

"More like a file cabinet or two."

I let out a groan. "Okay, have those sent to me and create one of those Cloud accounts so that I can get access to all the computer files she left."

"I'm not joking when I say it's a file cabinet's worth," Jenna said.

"Fine, just ship the whole file cabinet. How soon do you think you can have it here?"

There was silence on the other end of the call for at least a full minute.

"I honestly have no idea. I will start making phone calls as soon as my receptionist is in and I can focus on this. In the meantime, send me the address you would like me to have this shipped to."

"Fine," I agreed. I ended the call and headed downstairs to the hotel lobby and the concierge desk.

"Good morning." The concierge smiled brightly at me. "How can I help you today?"

"I'm having a couple of boxes of files delivered in the next day or two.

I was wondering if the hotel has executive office space that I can borrow and set up in as I sort through some paperwork?"

"We do have office spaces available for our guests. However, those are only available on an hourly basis. Sounds to me like you might want someplace where you can spread out and close the door behind you. Is that right?" she asked.

I hadn't really thought about what I needed. This was the type of thing I would typically have handed over to Alayna, and she would have provided me with a perfect solution.

"Yes, that sounds about right," I said.

"We have several flexible office solution locations in Seattle. Those are the kind of places where you can basically rent an office space, not unlike getting a hotel room," she told me.

"Is that something you could help me find?"

"Absolutely. What was your name again, sir?"

"Kyle Love."

She turned to her computer and her fingers flew over the keyboard. "I see you have an open-ended stay with us… and I have your room number here. How many days do you think you would want your office for?"

"I'm not exactly sure," I admitted.

"I'll put down that something open-ended would be preferred. And your location, is there a particular part of town you need?" Her fingers flew over the keyboard. "I have just a few more questions before I can get started. We've already discussed that you want an office where you can close the door, that will be a private office. Are you planning on having meeting, or will you need access to a conference room?"

"Not this time, just a workspace."

"Okay," she said as she continued to type. "How many desks and chairs, or people, will you need in your office?"

"Right now, it's just me, but I might need to bring an assistant in, so I guess enough space for two people to sort through a lot of files. And some place close to the hotel, I think, would be best for now."

"It looks like I should be able to find some availability. When do you want to start? Is this something you would want for today?"

I shook my head. "I don't think I'm going need it before tomorrow at the earliest."

She looked up from her typing. "I should be able to get this reserved for you. I can put your reservation through the hotel, and it will show on your bill with us. Will that work for you?"

"Yes, that would be fine," I said. The easier, the better as far as I was concerned.

"Fabulous. I will reach back out to you as soon as I have booked a space and have that confirmation."

I thanked her and started to walk away. She seemed competent. I turned around and stepped back to the desk.

"Mr. Love, you're back."

"You aren't looking for a new job, are you?" I asked.

"No sir, I am well situated here. What can I help you with?"

"I need a new personal assistant."

She didn't even seem fazed by my request. "I can do a little research for you and maybe locate a placement agency that would have an executive assistant with the proper skillset for you."

"You can do that?"

"This is a full-service concierge service. It may take a little longer than making arrangements for your office space, but yes, I can do that. I'll reach out and leave a message for you when I have some information."

I scratched my head as I turned to walk away. She was on top of things. She was exactly the kind of person I needed to replace Alayna. I turn back around. "Are you sure you don't want a job?"

She laughed politely and again declined my offer. I walked outside and found a local coffee shop to start my day.

With a hot coffee, I started to think a little clearer. I had an office lined up, even if it was just temporary. An assistant was potentially in my future if that concierge was as good as I expected her to be. I needed to find something more permanent than the hotel.

I texted Clarissa. *I'm looking for an apartment or a townhouse out here. What would be a good neighborhood* I asked. *I would like to be close to you and Leo.*

I sat and watched my phone, waiting for Clarissa to respond.

Are you serious? You're really going to stay in Seattle? When I saw her text, my heart actually sped up. At that point, I realized I had expected her to not answer me.

I will be wherever you and Leo are from now on.

What about your offices in Chicago and Hong Kong?

I wanted to be able to call her, or better yet, sit down and have a conversation.

Can we have dinner for a real conversation and not just texting back-and-forth?

The truth was I didn't know what I was going to do about my offices in Chicago or Hong Kong. Right now, I didn't really care. All of my focus and all of my desires were to get Clarissa back. This felt like one of those times when I would go into hyper-focus on a project, only for once, I didn't have Alayna as my backup, making sure the rest of my life didn't fall apart.

And here I was with my life falling apart with too many pieces for me to be able to solely focus on only one aspect of it. However, my main priorities at the moment were Clarissa and Leo.

Chicago and Hong Kong are in capable hands. What about that dinner? I asked.

I'll think about it.

It was a reasonable response even if it isn't what I wanted to see. I was surprised when she sent another text.

The neighborhood around the coffee shop where we last met is a good one. Maybe an apartment there would suit your needs.

35

CLARISSA

Several weeks later

Kyle seemed to have been true to his word when he said he was staying in Seattle. Not that I reached out to him, but he shared with me the results of his attempting to find a local apartment nearby. And he asked me to dinner at least once a week.

I know how Leo feels about dinosaurs. What are his thoughts on the zoo?

I smiled as I read Kyle's text. He was definitely trying to engage with us in a family positive manner. If he was finally willing to admit that he was Leo's father, it didn't seem fair that I withheld that relationship from our son.

Leo loves the zoo. He also likes the Museum of Natural History, I texted back.

I didn't even know Seattle had one.

There's also a pretty terrific science center here, but we can't do both in one day. That's too much stimulation. Both have dinosaurs, I informed him.

Which would you prefer? Kyle asked.

I had to think about that for a minute. Was I really discussing meeting Kyle for an outing with Leo again? In the end, we arranged to meet at the science center.

I didn't tell Leo exactly what we were doing, leaving the meeting Kyle part as a surprise on the off chance that he actually didn't show up, I didn't want to disappoint my baby that way. However, Kyle was there waiting for us.

"There's my b—" he started as he crouched down low and held his arms out.

I caught his eye and shook my head.

"Buddy!" Kyle changed gears on what he was saying rather quickly. "I missed you," he said as he swung our son up into his arms.

Leo squirmed and giggled with excitement.

Kyle leaned close to me as I stepped up to the two of them and unexpectedly gave me a quick kiss on the cheek.

"You haven't told him?" he asked in low tones.

I shook my head. "You weren't ready. I decided it would be better to wait," I confessed.

"You can tell him at any time now. I know I made a mistake by not letting you do so before."

"I'll think about it," I said as we walked into the science center. I wanted Leo to know that Kyle was his father. I also needed to protect my son. I still wasn't certain about Kyle's determination to be there for us. After all, he had left without warning twice before.

"I noticed we're right next to the Space Needle," Kyle pointed out.

"Maybe if we get done here and somebody isn't too tired, we could take a ride to the top." I hadn't yet done many of the touristy things since we moved, but it sounded like a fun idea to me.

What I thought was going to be a long morning looking at interactive exhibits and planetarium shows turned out to be much more engaging, and we were there for hours longer than I had expected. I knew Leo was done for the day when he started to fall asleep on his feet. As soon as I hauled Leo into my arms, he went limp with sleep.

"Does he always do this?" Kyle asked.

He took Leo from me. It wasn't fair. Leo was a sturdy kid and getting harder to carry every day, but Kyle made him look as if he weighed nothing more than a feather. I wasn't jealous that Kyle was carrying the boy, only that he managed to do so with ease.

"I think when he gets excited, he just expends his energy faster," I said. "He was excited to see you today."

"We had a good time today, didn't we?" Kyle asked.

"I think he only falls asleep around you," I said teasingly. "He never seems to run out of energy when it's just me." My son was exhausted. I was glad he had a good day and that he and Kyle seemed to be getting along well.

"Last time, you took our boy home and let him take a nap before I met you for dinner. I have to confess I'm not ready for the day to be over just yet. Is that something that you might be open to doing again?"

"Yes." I didn't even have to think about it before I agreed.

"There's a little sandwich and soup shop in the neighborhood. If you haven't tried it yet, we could meet there for dinner."

Kyle stayed with us until the car I arranged for arrived. My insides started doing flips on the ride home. Not big ones, but little ones, letting me know that I really wanted to see Kyle again.

Maybe this time, everything would work out, and I should let it happen.

Maybe this time, he would disappoint me and I would be left broken hearted again. I was having a hard time getting over his past rejection.

As a single mother with a small child, I was very aware and conscious of not maintaining the stereotype of always being late. I hadn't yet decided whether Kyle's constant ability of being at a place when we arrived was his attempt at trying to be present or some commentary on my ability to be anywhere when I said I would be. He was waiting at the restaurant when we arrived.

"I've walked past this place more times than I care to admit," he said, "and I never realized what kind of food they would have."

"Leo likes it, and he can be a picky eater," I said.

We ordered off the menus—large chalkboards hanging behind the counter—and carried a table number and our empty paper cups to a table. I grabbed a booster chair for Leo and got him situated. Kyle took our cups and returned with drinks from the self-service counter.

"Is that how you pick most of the restaurants you go to?"

"That's how I pick all the restaurants I go to," I confessed. "There's no point in taking him somewhere if he can't or won't eat. We don't eat out very often. I Mostly cook."

"That's why Friday is always spaghetti," he said with a chuckle.

"You remembered?" I found myself smiling more in Kyle's presence than I had been in the previous weeks.

He glanced down at the table before locking his piercing blue gaze with mine. "I remember everything, Clarissa."

He was so intense at that moment that I had to look away. I blinked, dashing away the sudden appearance of unexpected tears. If he remembered, why couldn't he commit to staying around?

The moment only lasted like a lightning bolt, sudden, hot, and gone with only an after image burned into my mind.

"I thought it was good for kids to eat the same foods their parents eat," he said as if he hadn't just driven a nail into my soul.

"It is, however, his palette isn't overly sophisticated or developed yet. It's going to take him some time before he's ready to venture into all the amazing food that is out there for him."

Kyle looked down at a grumpy Leo. "Did you have a good nap?"

Leo whined and shifted in his seat, turning his back to Kyle.

"Somebody," I said with a heavy sigh, "didn't have much of a nap today. He woke up about halfway home."

Kyle nodded in understanding. At least I hope he understood. After a brief moment of severe cranky attitude where I reminded Leo that we would go home if he didn't calm down, he immediately fell asleep with his hand in his food.

Kyle chuckled. "I should let you take him home," he said.

"There's no rush. He's already asleep," I pointed out before taking another bite of dinner. "He'll be fine." I reached out and cleaned Leo's hand before adjusting his position so that he would be more comfortable and not accidentally flop into his food. "We can finish dinner."

"That's good. I haven't had good company like yours in a long time. I appreciate your staying."

I tried not to blush, but I was very aware that I'd failed miserably.

Kyle reached out across the table. His fingers brushed the back of my hand.

My insides did that thing I hadn't felt in a long time. It was desire. I still wanted Kyle, even after all the pain he had caused me. And from his hooded gaze, I was pretty certain he wanted me. He wasn't sticking around simply to be a father to Leo.

I knew that's what he was trying to prove to me, that he could be a father to our son and that he wanted to. But it was nice to know that I was wanted as well.

The restaurant had bright lighting and could not be described as romantic, but at that moment, we might as well have been sitting in a secluded corner of a dimly lit, high-end, exclusive fine dining establishment. I had tunnel vision. All I saw was Kyle, and all I felt was the way he was stroking my hand.

"We should do this again," Kyle suddenly suggested with a clearing of his throat.

"I would like that," I admitted. I liked seeing him and Leo together. I thought it was good for both of them. But I also liked those moments of lightning between us. Would they come back?

"Here, let me get him," Kyle said, picking up the sleeping child. "Do you need me to get you a car? You aren't planning on walking, are you?"

I already had my phone out and was requesting a car through the app on my phone. I held it up to show Kyle. "I'm good. Would you like to go to the zoo with us next weekend?"

The smile he gave me was all the answer I needed.

36

KYLE

"Steve?" I heard Clarissa's voice.

"Oh, hi, Clarissa. What the hell are you doing here? Who's the kid?" Steve responded.

"Kyle asked us to meet him here for lunch. Um…"

"I'm back here," I called out as I shifted a stack of boxes.

She had Leo by the hand and looked a little confused when she walked toward the back of the new office space.

"I wasn't expecting all of this." She gestured at all the activity.

Jeremy, my new assistant, stopped with an armful of boxes. "Where do you want these?"

I glanced up and scanned the label on the side of the box. It took me a second to decipher the scrawl. Whoever packed the box had bad handwriting. "You can put those in that back corner office for now."

Steve walked past carrying a box of his arms. "What do you think of Kyle's new office?"

"Chaotic," Clarissa said. "I didn't know it was going to be more than just him and Jeremy. So, you just moved to Seattle?" she asked.

"I go where the job takes me," Steve yelled as he walked away.

"What happened to the office you had at that shared workspaces place?" she asked.

"I'm setting up a decent Seattle location while I figure out what to do with Chicago. I couldn't stay at that workspaces place. It was not cost efficient. And this is closer to the apartment."

"What about Hong Kong?"

"Hong Kong is good, and I trust Sullivan to be able to handle things in my absence. I'll probably have to go check on them in person for a week next quarter. I realize they don't really need me to be there all the time. After all, the whole point of setting up multiple international offices was so that I could travel and not be stuck in one place all the time."

"That makes more sense than relocating every time you think there's a problem with a client," she said.

Clarissa mentioning my past actions was not a dig. She hadn't mentioned it to remind me of my faults. She mentioned it because it had happened. This was a huge leap forward in my regaining her trust.

"Are you moving everybody out here or just Steve?" she asked.

"For now Steve, Jeremy, and I will be going back-and-forth to Chicago as needed. Michelle needs to be able to focus and get her renderings done without being interrupted by travel. We are still discussing whether I keep a full office in Chicago or if she'll continue to work remotely."

"But she's staying in Chicago with her family, right?" Clarissa asked.

"That's what we're working out. Everything is digital, anyway."

"What about the rest of the office? What about Phillip, James, and Jenna?"

I understood her concern. After all, she had worked with these people for a long time.

"James is more than ready to step away from consulting and embrace retirement. Jenna is willing to manage the office if we keep one there," I said.

"What are you thinking of doing?" she asked.

"I'm thinking that I need to be where you are. If that means I'm the remote satellite office here with headquarters in Chicago and Hong Kong, so be it. But there's some exciting stuff coming out of Seattle, and I think I'd like to see what's happening here."

"Really? You're going to stay because of us?"

I nodded. "I need to be where you are." I shifted my focus to Leo. "And you are here for lunch, aren't you?"

She let go of his hand, and he launched himself at me. I swung him up into my arms and braced him on my hip. "I'm starving. Where should we go?"

"I want sushi," Leo demanded.

"Since when do you like sushi?" I asked.

"They have been ordering sushi delivery at least once a week since Davey got here. Apparently, Leo loves the little sliced rolls. They are kid-sized. I had no idea he liked" —she mouthed the word for fish— "I don't think he knows exactly what he's eating."

"I haven't had sushi in a long time. That sounds like a great idea." I carried Leo toward the front looking for Jeremy to let him know we were leaving. Instead, we ran into Steve.

"We're heading out to lunch," I announced.

Steve looked up. "Okay. Hey, cute kid. Is that—"

"Steve, I want you to meet Clarissa's son, Leo."

Steve brushed off his hands on the sides of his jeans and extended one to the little guy. Leo, in all seriousness, shook hands and said, "Nice to meet you."

I ruffled his hair.

"We'll be back soon. I have no idea where the closest sushi place is," I admitted.

"Don't worry. I've got one pulled up on my phone. Looks like there's one just around the corner, and it has a five-star rating."

"Sounds good to me," I said as I put Leo on his own two feet and took his hand.

"I guess," Clarissa started. "It's not going to be much of a secret about us in this location anymore?"

"I'm sure everybody back in Chicago has already figured out you're why I'm staying here." I chuckled. "However, they don't know about…" I tilted my head in Leo's direction.

"Well, they do now," she said. "Steve is certainly not going to keep that a secret."

"But I introduced him as your kid," I pointed out.

Clarissa laughed. "Of course you did after he saw the two of you together. I saw his face. He definitely noticed the similarity between the two of you."

It hadn't occurred to me that other people would see the resemblance.

"How's work?" I asked, changing the subject.

"I am very much enjoying it. They haven't given me reason to complain about anything yet."

"I don't think I have ever heard you complain about any of your jobs," I pointed out.

"That's because you weren't around when I was a waitress. I absolutely hated that."

"When were you a waitress?" I asked.

"You were in Hong Kong."

There was a drop in her tone, and that was my fault. It wasn't Clarissa's place to get over that hurt. It was my job to try and make up for the pain I caused her. That was a lesson learned the hard way.

"That's why you're so good to wait staff," I said.

"I never want to be like the jerks I had to deal with, so, yes. When Leo makes a mess, I tip extra."

"Noted. I will make sure that I'm paying better attention when we go out. It's the very least I can do."

She slid her arm through mine and hugged it.

"Thank you," she said.

I wasn't necessarily going to apologize every time it came up, but I wanted her to know that I was aware of my culpability and that I would constantly work toward making things up to her in the best way I could.

The sushi place was the kind where everybody working shouted out a greeting when we stepped in the door. Leo randomly yelled something in return. I have no idea what he thought he was saying, but the head sushi chef behind the counter laughed.

I expected Clarissa to order something basic like a California roll or a cucumber roll for Leo. She said he seemed to like the fish, so I shouldn't have been surprised when she ordered him a spicy tuna roll. I ordered a variety for myself, and Clarissa ordered a tempura Bento box.

"I thought you liked sushi? I asked.

She shook her head and pointed to Leo. "He does, and Davey too. I still haven't developed those taste buds yet."

"What are your plans for this evening?" I asked when lunch was over and we stepped back outside. It was a lovely early spring day, and the constant overcast winter gloom had given away to blue skies and sunshine.

"We have some errands to run this afternoon, but nothing is going on. Ending Spring Break on a quiet note. It's school again on Monday."

"Tonight's Friday," I pointed out. "Doesn't that mean you are already booked for spaghetti and a movie?"

Clarissa laughed. "You're right," she said. "It is. I guess my plans are set. What are you doing tonight?"

"I will be working late, getting everything set up in the office I chose. I'd like to have us up and running by Monday. I need to get some actual work done before Steve heads back to Chicago. He's going back-and-forth to provide continuity between Phillip and me."

"I think you just like to have someone willing to be at your beck and call. We both know there's no reason for Steve to be taking drawings back-and-forth to Chicago when all of your work is done digitally."

"You have a point, but he seems to think this is what he wants to do for now."

"He is such a fanboy. After all, he followed you all the way to Hong Kong and now he's out here with you," she teased.

I wasn't going to deny her claim, but Steve was an excellent architect, and I was happy enough to have him working for me, whatever that capacity looked like.

"That means you're busy all day tomorrow too, doesn't it?" she asked.

"I'm afraid so," I admitted. "Why, what did you have in mind?"

She shrugged. "I thought maybe you would consider taking Leo for the day so I could get some stuff done around the house."

I looked down at the top of Leo's head. "Hey," I said, shaking his hand to get his attention. He turned his eyes that were so much like mine up at me. "How do you feel about hanging out with me and the guys in the office tomorrow?"

Leo's jaw dropped open. "Can I, Mommy?"

I followed his gaze to Clarissa.

"That would be okay with me. Are you sure you're okay with babysitting?"

I stopped walking and made sure that Clarissa was looking me in the eyes.

"It's not babysitting when it's Leo."

Her entire face lit up as she understood what I was saying. I knew she hadn't told Leo yet who I was, but I would be there to help parent our child when she needed me to be. I was more than honored that she finally trusted me to take care of our boy.

37

CLARISSA

I flopped back on the couch with a tired sigh. Our house was so much cleaner than it had been since before Davey and the movers brought all of our furniture months ago. I hadn't had proper time without everyone in the house to do the deep clean on the carpet and in the kitchen that I had been wanting to get done.

My phone pinged with a text message. *Oh my God, Clarissa! Davey booked us a bed and breakfast for the night. I did not realize we were going to be gone all weekend or I would have mentioned it earlier.*

That sounds wonderful, I responded.

It's so beautiful here and he's being extra romantic. Fingers crossed for you know what!'

Fingers crossed, I texted back.

Marci had been waiting for Davey to finally pop the question. Hopefully, this little weekend getaway would be when he finally got around to it.

Just let me know when you're headed back so that I'm not dancing around the house naked. Lol.

Marcy responded with three exclamation marks. *!!!You have a child!*

Child is hanging out with his father.

The phone rang.

"You're letting Kyle babysit?" Marci asked as soon as I picked up the phone.

"I'm letting Kyle try out his parenting responsibilities. If this is going to ever work out, he's going to have to be willing to do this sometimes," I said.

"And you trust him?" She sounded so skeptical.

I laughed. "I actually do, and Leo adores him. I think it's going to work out."

"As long as you're okay with it," she said.

"I'm okay with it. And you need to get back to your romantic weekend with Davey."

"One more thing," she said. "You aren't keeping a secret I should know about, are you?"

"First of all, no, I'm not. Second of all, if it was a secret, I wouldn't tell you because it's a secret. Now go have fun."

I ended the call and placed the phone on my stomach. I lay back and closed my eyes, enjoying the moment of peace and solitude. I don't know how long I lay like that before the phone rang again.

"Did he propose?" I asked without even looking at who was calling.

"I wasn't planning on it just yet, but if you want me to, I will," Kyle said with a chuckle.

I jumped into a sitting position, my pulse surging. "Oh, hi Kyle, I thought you were Marci." I laughed with embarrassment.

"Do I look like Marci?"

"When I'm not looking at the caller ID on my phone, you do."

He laughed even more. "Leo is getting pretty tired. I tried to get him to take a rest, but he refused. Too much going on. I guess it's time to come get him."

I didn't say anything for a long moment.

"Do you think you could bring him home?" I eventually asked.

"I don't know where you live. Are you sure you're ready for me to know this?"

I let out a long sigh. "I'm okay with you knowing where your son lives," I said. "I also think it's time that we sat down and told him, together."

"I like that idea," Kyle said. It sounded like he was smiling. "And what do we tell him when he asks why Mommy and Daddy don't live together?"

I groaned as I thought about his words. "Maybe that's something we figure out if he asks us."

"What do you want for dinner?" I asked.

"Are you cooking?"

"Hell no. I just spent my day alone scrubbing grout. I don't want to make any dirty dishes. I thought I might order something for delivery, and it should get here around the same time you do."

"That sounds like a dinner invitation," he practically purred.

"It is," I said.

"I've been eating nothing but pizza for days. I'm game for pretty much anything else. Burritos or hamburgers would be my top two."

"Okay, I will take it from here. I'll see you when you get home." I ended the call and immediately panicked. Kyle was coming over and going to see where I lived for the first time. My furniture didn't match, and we still had pictures resting on the floor against the wall because we ran out of hooks and hadn't bothered with getting more. The house and the neighborhood were nice, but we did not live in a high-rent zip code. At least everything was clean. I looked down at my sweaty and limp clothes. Everything was clean except for me.

Kyle's apartment and office were in the same neighborhood. That meant I had maybe fifteen minutes to take a shower and put on clean clothes. I managed to take a shower in record time and was pulling on a simple dress when the front door opened and Leo burst into the house. "Mommy, I am home!" he announced.

I was still toweling my hair off when I stepped into the living room. "Did you bring Kyle with you?"

"He did. I'm right here."

I could not suppress the grin that took over my face. "Well, this is it." I held my hand out in a very poor excuse for a presentation gesture.

Leo, who Kyle reported as being very tired, seemed to have found an untapped resource of energy and was bouncing on furniture and off the walls with excitement since Kyle was there.

"Why don't you show Kyle the rest of the house while I order dinner? You remember you cannot go into Davey's room or Marci's. Those are not your rooms to show."

"Okay." Leo nodded and dragged Kyle away.

The poor kid didn't even make it halfway through his order of chicken nuggets before he fell asleep and started to slide off the chair.

"I've got him," Kyle said as he scooped Leo up.

"Could you take his shoes off and put him in bed?" I asked.

"Do I need to do anything else?"

"Maybe next time you come over, we can go over the bedtime routine."

I swear that man smoldered at me. His eyes narrowed, and he got this not quite grin that crinkled the corners of his eyes and emphasized his cheekbones. I was positively giddy in his presence.

"So, where are your roommates?" Kyle asked when he returned.

"Davey announced that he was whisking Marci away for an impromptu day on the Sound. I thought he was just taking her out on a boat ride or something, but it seems to have turned into a romantic overnight at a bed and breakfast. I think he's finally going to propose."

"I thought they were already engaged," Kyle said.

"They were only unofficially engaged."

"Meaning?" He lifted his brows.

"Meaning they talked about it, and everybody knew they were going to get married, but nothing official has been done."

"Is that something you would want?" Kyle asked.

"What do you mean?" I asked.

"Would you want to know that you would be getting engaged at some point in time, or do you want it to be a complete surprise?"

I looked at him and bit my lip. I had to think about that for a minute or two. "Maybe at one point, I would have wanted the perfect surprise engagement. Too much life has happened since then. I have a little boy I have to take care of and protect."

"You're doing a fantastic job with him," Kyle said.

"Thank you. He changes everything. I think if I were to be with somebody who wanted to marry me, I would want to know. I know it doesn't sound very romantic. Maybe knowing that we're both interested and want to go forward with our lives together is romantic enough."

"Fair enough. Then you should know that I intend on proposing at some point," he said with all seriousness.

I blinked, uncertain of where this conversation was going. "This is all hypothetical, right?" I laughed nervously.

"For tonight it is," Kyle said. "You know I plan on being in Leo's life, and ideally, that would mean that you're in mine."

I'm not sure how I melted or when, but I got out of my seat and crawled into Kyle's lap. I placed my hand against the side of his cheek and stared deeply into his eyes, something I had longed to do for countless months.

"You have to stop breaking my heart before I think I could say yes."

"But you think you could say yes?"

I couldn't speak as I got lost in the intensity of his eyes. I bit my lip and nodded.

Kyle closed his eyes and lowered his head to kiss me, and then I closed my eyes and got lost in the sensation of his lips against mine.

Kyle stood, effortlessly lifting me. His chair fell back to the floor with a loud crash.

I giggled. "Where do you think you're taking me?"

"Our son gave me a very thorough tour of the house, including showing me Davey's computer room. We did not go into Marci's bedroom, but Leo opened her door to show me. By the way, your roommates are slobs."

"He didn't," I said, burying my head against Kyle's shoulder.

"Don't worry, I made sure to close the doors after he pushed them open, announcing that we couldn't go in, but we stayed in the hallway. He also showed me your room, which he took me into."

"You put him up to that," I teased.

"I didn't have to. But I noticed this house is old and solidly built with nice, thick walls."

Kyle's smile was like a wolf's, predatory and full of teeth.

38

KYLE

It felt like a miracle to have Clarissa back in my arms.

Her sighs drove me mad like some kind of hyped-up sex drug. Her lips were an aphrodisiac, and I was her willing addict. I set her on her bed and stared at the goddess that she was.

"I've missed you, Clarissa."

She held my hand, intertwining our fingers.

"I've missed you." Her voice was almost a whisper.

"Tell me to go if you don't want this," I said. I clenched my gut, prepared for the knife of her words to plunge into my chest.

"Kyle," she started. She climbed up onto her knees. "I've always wanted you, and that's the scary part of all of this. I can't hate you. Please promise me that you won't try to hurt me again."

I brushed tears from her cheeks. "I will never hurt you again. I love you, Clarissa. I know I've been an idiot and I don't deserve you, but I swear I will spend every day for the rest of my life earning back your trust."

She leaned in and pressed her softness against me.

I wrapped my arms around her, pulling her body tight against mine. Her lips danced across mine. I skimmed my hands over the fabric of her dress, her curves and warmth teasing my palms.

"Stay," she pleaded. "Stay with me."

"Forever," I growled as I clutched her. She was mine, and I would never be the same fool I had been before. I would never let this woman go.

I bunched the thin fabric of her dress into my fists and pulled it over her head.

It had been far too long since I had touched her. Her skin was the softest my fingers had ever been graced with being allowed to touch.

She grabbed the front of my waistband and fought with the button on my jeans.

I didn't want to be separated from her, not even for a second, but I had to step away long enough to pull my shirt off and unfasten my jeans.

Clarissa dragged me back to her. Her breasts pressed against my chest, and she ran her hands under the waistband of my jeans and boxers, pushing my jeans to the floor.

She tasted so sweet and felt a thousand times better than that.

I pressed her back onto the mattress as I somehow kicked my pants the rest of the way off. I couldn't believe my luck that she was welcoming me into her bed, back into her arms. I trailed kisses over her jaw and down her neck. I wanted to savor every lick, every taste. I lost my ability to restrain myself once I sucked a dusky nipple into my mouth.

She gasped and arched up to me. Her breasts were so round and soft. I lost myself, pressing into her while pulling and tugging on the nipple in my mouth.

Clarissa weaved her fingers through my hair, clutching me to her. Her legs slid against mine, and she wrapped those amazing thighs around my hips.

The warmth of her core teased my cock. I was hard and aching to be inside her.

"Kyle, please."

There was something about her begging that undid me. I wanted to take my time with her, but I was as desperate as she was.

I plunged into her wet pussy. I stopped breathing. Her body was everything. She was home, she was love, she was magic. I found my breath again as my hips pulled back before sliding back into her.

She let out a whimper. She grabbed onto me harder.

I sucked her further into my mouth and kneaded her other breast with increased vigor. She was mine, and this was the most intense need I had ever felt for her. Every time with her was better than the time before.

Her inner walls clenched and released in a perfect dance that drove me to a frenzied pace. She matched me thrust for thrust, drawing me ever deeper into her body, into her being.

The sounds she made let me know she was close to her orgasm moments before her body told me. She didn't know what to hold onto. She grabbed my hair, my arms, and she pounded her fists against the bed. Her inner walls began bouncing off my cock without rhythm or rhyme.

I growled with great joy as she lost it. Her head fell back, and she struggled to gasp for air as the orgasm rolled over her.

"Don't… don't stop," she begged.

It was hard. I didn't want to stop, but her body was literally sucking my own orgasm out of me. I wasn't going to have any muscle control in a matter of seconds.

This was for her as much as it was for me, maybe even more so. She deserved all the good feelings, all the orgasms first. I fought to maintain control of my body. She let out a keening whine as something intense tightened all of her muscles. I was no longer in control as my body spilled into her. I felt as if my entire body was turning to liquid before I was back in my own skin.

I fell to the side, pulling her into my arms and holding her tightly.

"I love you," she said between panting breaths.

"I love you. I have missed what you do to me," I confessed.

Morning light woke me. I eased out of bed, letting Clarissa sleep. I got dressed and went to kiss her and let her know I was leaving.

She grabbed my hand. "You don't have to go."

I glanced over my shoulder in the direction of Leo's room.

"I don't think he'll make anything of it as long as we treat it as being normal," she said. "He'll be happy to see you. Stay at least through breakfast."

"If I'm staying for breakfast, then I will make pancakes for everyone."

With a stretch that did amazing things to her breasts, Clarissa asked, "You make pancakes?"

"And I'm very good at it," I confessed. I could not help myself, I leaned in and palmed one of her perfect breasts while I kissed her thoroughly.

I was in the kitchen working on breakfast with bacon sizzling on the stove and ladling pancake batter onto an electric skillet when Leo discovered I was still there. He came running into the kitchen and wrapped himself around my legs.

"Careful there, kiddo," I said. "I'm cooking."

"You sound just like Mommy," he said. "She says that when she's cooking and doesn't want me to get hurt."

"That is exactly right," I said.

"Are you making pancakes? I love pancakes," he said.

"Me too," I agreed. "Is your mommy up?"

"She's in the bathroom."

Okay, I could do this. I didn't have to worry about what to feed him. I could ask. "Do you drink milk or orange juice with breakfast?"

It seemed odd that my son was almost six, and I had no idea whether he even drank milk.

"Milk makes my tummy hurt," he said.

I paused and looked at him. "Really? Mine too." I was fine with processed dairy, but not milk. "Does cheese give you a tummy ache?" I asked.

"No. They get mad at me sometimes at school because everybody has to drink milk except for me."

"What do you drink at school?"

"Water or juice boxes," he said.

There was so much about him that I didn't know, and it felt like I should, such as his lactose intolerance.

"Are there foods you can't have, like peanuts?"

"My friend Declan is allergic to peanuts. His mommy won't let him even have candy with them."

"But your mommy lets you have peanuts?"

"I can't have peanut butter and jelly sandwiches at school because it will make Declan very, very, very, very"—he kept saying very— "sick, and I don't want to make Declan sick."

"That sounds like you're being a good friend, keeping him from getting sick. What does Mommy drink?"

"Mommy likes coffee," he said and then proceeded to make a face. Clearly, he didn't like coffee. The conversation felt a little surreal, but then again, most conversations with Leo were not anything I could have expected.

"Good morning," Clarissa mumbled as she staggered into the kitchen, her hair a sexy mess, and she had put on a pair of comfortable looking pajamas that I found to be sexier than I think she intended them to be. Then again, it was Clarissa who was exceptionally sexy this morning. "Oh, coffee, good." She went straight to the coffee maker and poured herself a cup.

"Leo was telling me that milk gives him a tummy ache," I said.

She padded across to where I stood in front of the stove and stared down at the food.

"That looks delicious," she said. "I hope that it tastes as good as it smells. Yeah, he can't have milk. He seems to be okay with ice cream, yogurt, and cheese, and anything that's been processed."

"I'm that way too," I said.

She stopped and stared at me for a moment before shrugging. "I guess that makes sense because he certainly didn't get that from me."

Her phone rang. She picked it up from where she had left it charging the evening before.

"Oh, crap!"

"What's wrong?" I asked.

"Marci and Davey are headed back earlier than I expected," she said, "and…" She read the front of her phone. "It looks like things did not go the way Marci wanted them to. They are headed back early."

"That sounds like I'll be heading out right after breakfast," I said.

"Thank you for understanding."

I spent the rest of the day thinking about how disappointed her friend must have been when she was expecting a proposal. I needed to make sure that I did not let Clarissa down that way ever again. However, on Monday morning, I received a message that had me worried that I might. Sullivan sent a lengthy email from the Hong Kong office explaining how the client for a new building wanted me on hand.

Sullivan was perfectly capable of handling the client's every need. I needed to be here for Clarissa and Leo. She would never, ever forgive me if I left now. I knew this was my last chance at winning the woman I loved and keeping her in my life.

39

CLARISSA

A few weeks later

"Ready to go see Daddy?" I asked Leo as I picked him up from daycare.

"Can we?" He launched to his feet and ran to get his jacket and backpack that were all lined up by the door and ready to go.

Kyle was officially "Daddy" now. I had been nervous letting Leo know, but no more nervous than letting Kyle back into my heart. And Kyle was doing everything right these days. Even when it made him grouchy. He had been moody for almost a month over this Hong Kong trip. Why did it always come back to Hong Kong?

Steve was on the phone and waved as we walked past. And as I suspected, once he saw Kyle and Leo, our past was no longer a secret. But now that we were officially a couple, everyone back in Chicago knew Kyle and I obviously had a history and that we were back together.

I let go of Leo's hand so he could run to his father, like he did every time we saw Kyle. It was becoming a bit of a routine. After work, I picked up Leo, we would walk the few blocks to Kyle's office two or three times a week, and on Fridays, Kyle came home with us for a big spaghetti dinner and a movie.

I saw Kyle waving at Leo before I noticed he was on the phone. My gut tightened as I anticipated the growl, the tears, a scene that I had seen in movies where the kid didn't know, and the parent yelled and was mean. I was prepared to sweep in and rescue my son.

But none of that happened.

Kyle put his index finger over his lips to quiet Leo down before pulling him up on his lap. As he kept talking, he placed paper and a pen in front of our son, ruffled Leo's hair, and kissed his head.

Leo was perfectly content to just be with his father, even though Kyle's attention was elsewhere. My heart clenched and grew, and I had to blink away tears. Kyle Love had always been a magnetic force, and I had always been swept away with him like being dragged along in a current. But this version of him constantly surprised and amazed me.

On the day we agreed to tell Leo, Kyle had shown up with matching T-shirts wrapped in a gift box.

"So we can match the next time we go to the zoo!" he announced.

I cried that day too.

He hung the phone up with an annoyed growl.

Leo flinched.

"Sorry, Son," he said, giving Leo a quick hug.

"You look like you're going to be working late," I said.

Kyle nodded. "The client is getting pushier about my being present for the ground breaking."

I didn't want Kyle to leave for the very traumatizing reason that I didn't know whether he would come back. But we both had to compromise to make this work.

"Why don't you go?" I asked.

"Clarissa, I've told you. I'm not going to leave you and Leo."

"I know that," I said with a heavy sigh.

Kyle's brows lifted and he pointed at me. "I saw that. Your words say one thing, but your heart doesn't really believe that. I have to heal your hurt so your heart will know I will always come back to you. Until then, I'm here."

Leo held up his drawing. "Look, a lion!"

"Oh, that's beautiful," I said, grateful for a moment of distraction. "Why don't you go show that to Mr. Steve? I'm going to talk to Daddy for a minute."

Leo squirmed off Kyle's lap. He held his masterpiece in front of him as he ran out of the office.

Kyle was grinning as he watched Leo run off.

"What?" I asked.

"I love that. I never knew that having him call me Daddy would fill me with such emotion. Every time. Please tell me it doesn't get old."

I laughed. "Having Leo call me Mommy is amazing, until it's not. And then it's annoying. But the magic returns and it's amazing again. I'm really glad you like it. It suits you."

Kyle started to narrow his gaze.

"Stop that. We are not having that Daddy word conversation right now."

It was Kyle's turn to laugh.

"Look, I know you don't want to leave us. And I don't think you will. Alayna made sure of that. I will forever be grateful to her for quitting."

Kyle started to open his mouth. I held my hand out to stop him.

"She is an amazing woman, but I don't think she did you any favors," I continued. "You relied on her so much, and she picked up all the pieces you left in your wake. You needed to go to Hong Kong for a project. Instead of simply taking care of the task at hand and returning to whatever else you had going on, Alayna was behind you, enabling you to be distracted. With her as your professional sidekick — I don't think assistant is as all-encompassing as what she did for you—you were able to be a different version of you than you are now. I know it makes you nuts that Jeremy has boundaries and will not immediately answer the phone when you call during his non-work hours, but honestly, that's so much healthier for both of you. She may have been the most amazing person at that time and place. You were able to grow an international reputation. It's safe to say you wouldn't have gotten to where you are without her."

He nodded. "She was one of a kind. Still is."

"Yeah, absolutely. But on a personal level, you weren't able to have a relationship with me."

He started to protest.

I shook my head. "No. You were never going to be able to have a relationship with anyone for more than a few weeks here or there because you didn't have to maintain anything. You didn't even make sure your condo was cleaned or the electricity bills were paid. She made it so you could do whatever you wanted without ever having to look back. And honestly, if she hadn't figured out that there was something between us, she would have continued to be there for you in that capacity."

"What do you mean?"

"She got really pissed on my behalf when you left the last time, and she realized she was always having to put out the fires you left behind."

"She said that?" he asked.

"Not in so many words. Look, when I left Chicago, she seemed like a bottle rocket ready to explode. Part of me feels bad that she ever got to that level of frustration and disappointment. But only a little part. Because when Alayna went boom, you had to figure the rest of everything out fast."

"And boy, did she go boom. She chewed me out a few times before dropping the bomb that she was quitting. She quit on New Year's Eve after telling me how much I had let her down." Kyle stood and walked around his desk. He picked up my hands from where they rested in my lap.

"I love my job, you know that. I'm good at it, and I love watching my designs come to life. But you are the love of my life, and I was too wrapped up in myself to even realize it. And that is why I cannot go this time."

I squeezed his hands. "Kyle, that's why I think you should go. It's for a party, a photo op. A chance to shake hands and pat each other on the back. And here's the crazy part. You can get back on a plane and come home. You don't have to stay."

He let out a low groan. "I'll get there, and I'll see everything that I could be doing to fix it, and…"

"And then Jeremy will tell you to come home because you have an office here, with multiple locations and multiple architects who also need your expertise and guidance."

He pulled me out of the chair and into the space between his legs as he settled against the front edge of his sturdy desk. "Have I ever told you how smart you are? Do they have any idea of what a valuable asset they have in you at your job?"

As he wrapped his arms around my hips, I played with the buttons on the front of his shirt. "I think they might. I think you're pretty smart, too. Even if this whole Hong Kong thing makes you moody."

"I'm not moody." He practically pouted.

"Mommy!" Leo came running back into the office. "I want to go to King Kong."

"Go where?"

"King Kong! Mr. Steve said Daddy was going to see King Kong. I wanna go. I want to see the big gorilla."

Kyle started laughing. "Hong Kong. It's a part of China. There are no giant gorillas, not King Kong."

"I always thought Hong Kong was a city on an island with the same name," I said.

"It's more than a single city. There is a Hong Kong island, but there is more than that. You should see it someday." His eyes narrowed, and suddenly, a huge smile spread across his face.

"What?"

"I'm going to Hong Kong for the ground breaking," he announced. "And you and Leo are coming with me."

"Kyle?"

"How do you feel about a destination wedding? Let's do it. Come with me. Marry me. It'll be fun."

"I... I..." I didn't know what to say.

"This is where you say yes," Kyle teased.

I started panic laughing. "Leo doesn't have a passport. I need to ask for time off from work. There's so much to do."

Kyle kissed me. "Just say yes. We'll get the rest of the details figured out."

"Yes!" I pressed a kiss to his lips and held on tight.

40

EPILOGUE

KYLE

A *year later...*
Clarissa waddled from the car. Leo had already burst into Marci and Davey's house, eager to find the baby, while I waited for my beautiful wife as she carried our second child inside her. I had spent every moment by her side as soon as she told me she was expecting. I drank her in, memorizing every wonderful, awkward step.

"I'm coming as fast as I can," she complained.

"I didn't say anything," I said as I held my empty hands up.

"You didn't have to. Your face says it all," she said accusingly.

"And what is my face saying?"

She stopped walking and bit her lower lip. She sniffed and looked down at the ground.

I was off the stoop and by her side in an instant. "Whatever you're thinking, that's not what my face was saying. Clarissa, look at me, darling." I tipped her face up to mine with a finger under her chin.

I pressed a kiss to her soft lips.

"That translator you have in your head that thinks it can read my expressions is lying to you."

"You think I'm funny looking." She sniffed.

"I think you're gorgeous, a goddess on this earth."

"Really? Is that what you were thinking?"

"I was actually thinking about how I am so very happy to see you pregnant, and I was kicking myself for having missed this when you carried Leo. I don't want to miss a minute of your looking like this. And you're cute when you waddle."

"I'm waddling?" She started to cry.

I guided her head to my shoulder and wrapped her in my embrace.

"I'm a waddling watermelon. Why did I think a green striped dress was a good idea when I'm this pregnant?" she cried.

"You're a very cute watermelon. Now, come on. We're the last ones here. We need to get inside or they're going to wonder what's taking so long. Leo has already announced our arrival."

I wrapped my arm around her back and walked slowly with her. I knocked and then opened the door as we always had. So much in my life has changed since Clarissa. I was a husband, a father, and we had friends that were like family. Clarissa was the best thing to have ever happened to me, and I was still learning exactly what that meant.

"You're here!" Steve called out as we stepped inside. "Happy anniversary."

"Congratulations. Thanks for inviting us." Michelle from the Chicago office came up and gave Clarissa a hug. "I can't believe I waited so long to come out to Seattle. It's beautiful here. I can see why you moved."

"I thought you were here. Leo has already declared that no one is allowed on Brandon's blanket and has set up a guard station in the other room," Marci said as she walked past carrying a bowl full of chips.

We crossed through the room to where Leo sat next to the baby blanket on the floor. The blanket was Marci and Davey's son Brandon's clean, safe place to play. And as he grew more mobile with newly learned crawling skills, Leo was taking his keep-the-baby-on-the-blanket job very seriously. He had been given keeper of the baby duties a little over a week ago when we were over for our regular Friday night spaghetti dinner.

I grabbed Davey's shoulder and gave it a squeeze. "Thanks for hosting this for us, man."

"Are you kidding me? Marci would have my head on a platter if I didn't," he replied. "Beer is in the cooler on the back deck."

"Is that the brisket?" Clarissa asked. She closed her eyes and inhaled deeply. She followed her nose out through the next room and onto the back deck.

My wife had been craving smoked brisket for months. In an attempt to be a faithful, doting husband, I began asking everyone I knew if they had the proper skill set to smoke a brisket without turning it into charcoal or beef jerky. Which so far, had been the results of my failed attempts. I had no idea until that happened that Davey was some kind of grill master.

It was a no-brainer to ask him to help me out when it came to this little gathering, our first anniversary. Since I had whisked Clarissa to the far side of the planet to get married, this party—with the help of Marci and Davey—was the wedding reception we never had with our friends.

More people were gathered around outside. The weather behaved perfectly.

"No, I'm not handing him my phone right now. He's at a party," Jeremy was snapping into his phone, his face pinched. He pressed something on the phone and put it into his pocket. His eyes met mine. "Boundaries. I swear, you all need to learn boundaries."

"What did I do?" I asked. "I just got here."

He pulled his phone back out from his pocket and waved it at me. "That was Sullivan, calling me on a Saturday because you aren't emailing him back fast enough."

"It's like six a.m. there," I said. "And it's Sunday for him. Why is he calling?"

"I don't know, and you are not going to pick up your phone to check your work email right now. I think you set a bad precedent, and now he expects me to make sure that you are available twenty-four, seven. Buildings don't go up that fast. He can wait."

I had established some bad working habits. Then again, at that time, I didn't realize what a work-life balance was. I thought work was life, and then Clarissa happened, again. I wasn't sure if I believed in destiny, but it certainly seemed like fate wanted me and her to be together. Every time I messed up, I was given another chance for her love. I was lucky. Clarissa took me back, not once, but twice.

"That man needs to fall in love. Maybe then, he'll learn to appreciate that there is more to life than renderings and client meetings," I said.

"What are you talking about?" Clarissa asked. "I just heard you say there is more to life than client meetings. What did I miss?"

"Sullivan in Hong Kong is harassing me to get Kyle to call him back over the weekend," Jeremy said. "He wanted me to give him the phone, right now."

"And I was saying Sullivan needs to find something outside of work to make him happy."

Clarissa laughed. "You used to be the same way. He probably needs you to come to Hong Kong for some big client meeting."

I looked down at her. She was round with my baby. "I'm not going anywhere for a while."

"If I were not about to pop out the next generation of the Love family, I would say take me with you." She placed her hands on either side of her belly.

I skimmed mine over hers and gently caressed the top of her baby bump. "You want to go to Hong Kong for a meeting?"

"I wouldn't say no to having a chance at going back. We were married there, after all."

"I'm sure whatever Sullivan is getting anxious about can be dealt with over a video call on Monday morning. Because that's when I'll give him a call."

Clarissa looked wistful.

"What?"

"I remember a time when you would have been on the phone and getting plane tickets before you even knew what the problem was. They needed you, you went."

My gut clenched. At least she was able to joke about those bad choices I'd made. I leaned in and kissed her cheek. She knew I would forever be sorry that I had been so blind to the pain my actions had caused. Never again.

"That was a different time, a different me."

"Good," she said, giving me a bright smile that made her eyes twinkle. "I like this version of you a whole lot. You know Leo's school is almost out. Maybe we could go for part of the summer? You could take care of your clients, and I…" She let out a defeated sigh. "Will have just had a baby and will not want to do anything."

"Maybe not this year. But when the kids are older, that could be fun. Maybe we could go for an extended six months or a year?"

"Would this be a working extended stay? Because I think you need to take me too," Jeremy said. He held up his bottle. "Seriously, take me with you. I need more beer."

"My last assistant hated the idea," I said, watching him leave.

"She went, didn't she?" Clarissa added.

"Begrudgingly, and she hated every second of it. But seriously, would you be interested? Take the kids, live abroad for a while?"

She slid her arms around my waist. "What's the point of having an internationally renowned architect for a husband if I don't get to enjoy the international part?"

"And here I thought you were more interested in the architectural part," I teased.

"What?"

"You like my erections," I whispered in her ear.

"Mr. Love, you are incorrigible. But you're not wrong. You build things nicely."

I kissed the tip of her nose. "Mrs. Love, you are quite adorable. Happy anniversary."